HOUNDS OF HELL

"Why is it so quiet?" I asked Tarani.

The desert of Gandalara seems flat. Its hilly contours make themselves noticed in two ways—first, by the strain in your legs as you walk up and down the mounded sand; second, when something or someone, hidden by the gentle hills, appears as if from out of nowhere.

The dralda appeared now, too excited over the end of the hunt even to howl.

The dralda were dog-like in the same sense that the sha'um were cat-like—huge, with sharp tusks instead of teeth. This and a swift impression of the high-shouldered shape of a hyena combined with the size of a great dane were all I could tell about them before one slammed into me, knocking me backward with breath-killing force.

I could feel each of eight sharp claws pricking into my skin. Its head loomed over my face, its lips drawn back. A soft growl vibrated through its paws.

I turned my head cautiously. Tarani was pinned underneath the massive body of another. The remaining animals circled us, seemingly frustrated that their prey had been claimed. Then, from beyond Tarani, one lifted its head and began to howl...

THE WELL OF DARKNESS
Fourth Volume in the Gandalara Cycle
by Randall Garrett and Vicki Ann Heydron

THE GANDALARA CYCLE

IV
THE WELL OF DARKNESS

RANDALL GARRETT and VICKI ANN HEYDRON

BANTAM BOOKS
TORONTO · NEW YORK · LONDON · SYDNEY

THE WELL OF DARKNESS
A Bantam Book / December 1983

Map by Robert J. Sabuda

ISBN 0-553-23719-5

Published simultaneously in the United States and Canada

Bantam Books are published by Bantam Books, Inc. Its trade-
mark, consisting of the words ''Bantam Books'' and the por-
trayal of a rooster, is Registered in U.S. Patent and Trademark
Office and in other countries. Marca Registrada. Bantam
Books, Inc., 666 Fifth Avenue, New York, New York 10103.

PRINTED IN THE UNITED STATES OF AMERICA

H   0987654321

THE WELL OF DARKNESS

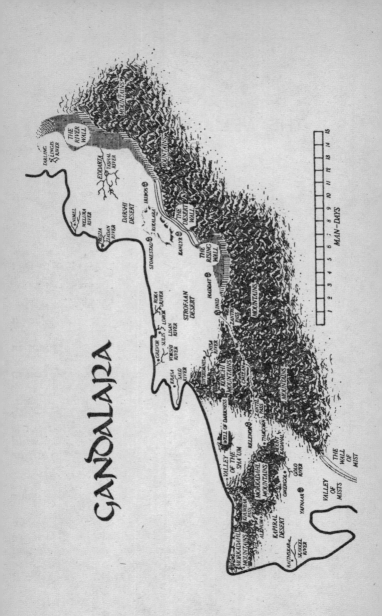

PRELIMINARY PROCEEDINGS: INPUT SESSION FOUR

—Enter, please. I see it is time to continue the Recording.

—Yes.

—You sigh. Are you not well?

—I'm fine, Recorder. But this part of the story is ... unpleasant for me to remember. To hate someone so much isn't something I'm proud of.

—Perhaps you judge yourself too harshly.

—Judge. You have told me, Recorder, that you only Record, that you do not judge. What of the All-Mind? Does it form judgments?

—That is a question I may answer in belief, but not in fact.

—I'd like to know what you think. Please, it is important to me.

—Very well, then. I believe that the All-Mind, too, merely Records. Only those who seek its knowledge make judgments about what they read there. I also believe it is your purpose, in making this Record, that all who would learn of these events you recount see as clear a truth as possible.

—That's true.

—And do you think that such a seeker would find your hatred unprovoked?

—No. Thank you, Recorder. I believe I can continue now.

—Good. Then, to quickly sum up what has gone before, we return to a point outside Eddarta. You and Keeshah and Tarani have the Ra'ira, a blue gem which confers telepathic powers on one who is already mindgifted. You have brought it

out of the city of rivers and slaves, and are taking it back to
Raithskar, where it may be properly safeguarded. Now make
your mind one with mine, as I have made mine one with the
All-Mind . . .

WE BEGIN!

1

I breathed a sigh of relief when the last of the farmland at the outskirts of Eddarta fell behind us.

It wasn't that I found the desert attractive—quite the opposite. Our hurried exit from the city hadn't allowed us time to bring provisions for the desert crossing, and Tarani and I could look forward to being slightly uncomfortable before we reached the nearest Refreshment House, where the Fa'aldu would provide us with food, water, and shelter.

Keeshah would have the worst of it, I was afraid. The big cat's body was even more efficient than ours at conserving water, but he was going to carry two people across nearly two hundred miles of hot, totally waterless desert. If I pushed him, we could make the trip in less than three days, but by the time we reached the Refreshment House at Iribos, he would be badly in need of food and rest.

The hardship ahead of us notwithstanding, being out of Eddarta was like no longer having a toothache. Now that we were safely out of Idomel's reach, I realized that I had felt oppressed and burdened during the time we had spent in Eddarta. The pressure to accomplish our purpose had contributed to that sensation, and my confused feelings for Tarani hadn't helped any. The city itself, however, had disturbed me—it had a character that was distinctly distasteful.

As Rikardon, I was a blending of the Gandalaran memories and abilities of a native with the perceptions and attitudes of a stranger. Ricardo, the stranger, viewed all Gandalaran things from the perspective of a twentieth-century American. Young Markasset, the native, hadn't known a whole lot about his own world. His strong points had been physical skills and emotion, not intellectual curiosity. He had been aware of the fact that slavery was practiced in Eddarta and had, in a general way, disapproved.

Eddarta, however, was all the way on the other side of Markasset's world from his home city of Raithskar, and both

3

cities had been centuries developing their styles. Slavery in Eddarta, though regrettable to Markasset, had seemed as much a fact of life as the beneficial bureaucracy ruled by the Council of Raithskar.

Ricardo Carillo, had studied languages for most of his life. Inseparable from that study was an awareness of the history through which languages developed and changed. Ricardo had a healthy respect for every man's right to choice; he had invested a few years of his life, through military service in the U.S. Marines, in support of that ideal.

Eddarta didn't fit directly into any historical pattern I could identify from human history, but it had the unpleasant elements of several unappetizing periods.

Revenue from land or service didn't belong to the producer, but to his or her "landpatron"—a member of one of the seven ruling families. In feudal Europe, the rise of the guilds had helped break down the feudal system. Crafts hadn't been tied to the land, and a Guildsman had been able to take his art out of range of an ungrateful sponsor.

Travel wasn't all that easy in Gandalara, where everyone except Sharith (which meant nearly everybody) *walked*, and every*where* they walked was mostly desert. In Eddarta, craftsmen continued to be identified by their work location, just like food producers. A part of their revenue went to their landpatrons, and craftsmen could be called upon for special service with no payment. If a Lord wanted to throw a special party, the fresh fruit and a new set of bronze tableware were equally available to him on request from his landservants.

The Lords of Eddarta, while unlikable, were no dummies. They knew better than to ask of the people on whom they depended for their comfort to do certain kinds of work for them. Slaves were bought, conquered, or condemned to do those jobs.

Besides being useful as personal servants and heavy laborers, the slaves provided Eddarta with a lowest class, so that the landservants could think of themselves as farmers or craftsmen or merchants. While the slaves were totally under the control of the Lords, landservants had the *illusion* of freedom, though they seldom tried to leave Eddarta.

Their freedom was a political illusion much like the psychic ones Tarani could project. I'm sure that my sense of relief

4

included a feeling of gratitude that we had never been truly a part of Eddarta, and so could truly escape the city.

At least *I* could.

I wasn't sure what *Tarani* was feeling, except that the heaviness of her body against my back told me of her weariness. She had managed to nap, now and again—a remarkable feat for one riding second place on a sha'um. I, at least, had the security of direct contact with Keeshah's furred back. Tarani's position, riding the cat's hips, her legs bent and tucked inside mine, was more precarious and less comfortable. That she had been able to sleep spoke eloquently of how tired she was.

We had been traveling for several hours, and had a substantial head start on any possible pursuit from Eddarta. The moon had set; since little starlight could penetrate the continuous cloud cover, Keeshah was finding his route through scent, memory, and an innate sense of direction. He ran through an eerie silence, his breathing and the whisper of sand under his big paws the only sounds we heard. He seemed tireless.

Stop, Keeshah, I said to the sha'um, through the telepathic linkage we shared.

No. Keeshah's thought was abrupt, preoccupied; his body continued its pace without hesitation.

What? Don't you want to rest? I asked him.

No. Again that scary sense of distance, as if he were responding automatically to a routine question that didn't really require his attention.

I had been half asleep myself, dozing with my face pressed into soft fur. The strangeness of Keeshah's mood pulled me fully awake.

Hey, I said. *It's been a long night, Keeshah. You may be indestructible, but we're not. Let's stop and catch a few hours' sleep.*

Don't want to, he said, finally focusing his attention on me.

Something was still strange, and it was a minute or two before I could pinpoint what it was. Keeshah seemed to be speaking to me from only the surface of his mind. Our usual close contact, that occurred on a deeper level as shared *thinking*, rather than shared *thought*, was closed off, blocked.

Is something wrong, Keeshah? I asked him.

Hesitation, then: *No.*

5

He must be more tired than he wants to show me, I decided. *He's hiding it because he's eager to get home*.

Me, too, I sighed. *Markasset loved Raithskar, but he hadn't seen much of the world. I haven't been everywhere in, Gandalara myself, but I've covered a large chunk of territory these past weeks, and I'm in a better position to appreciate Raithskar's beauty, cleanliness, and peacefulness*.

I thought of what lay within the leather pouch that rode within the crook of my hip. *After I deliver the Ra'ira to Thanasset—and take a week-long bath—I'm going to show Tarani the city. I know she'll love it as much as I do*.

Thoughts of Tarani reminded me of what Keeshah's odd mood had distracted me from: the need to get some rest.

Please stop, Keeshah, I said.

He didn't answer me for a few seconds, and I found myself considering the astonishing possibility that the big cat might refuse—something that hadn't happened since Markasset and Keeshah, both of them youngsters, had formed their unique bond.

Markasset may have *thought* that he gave Keeshah orders, but I'd never had that delusion. From the day I had awakened in Gandalara, I had been awed by the big cat, and delighted by our partnership. Keeshah had done some things that went against his own wishes, but out of friendship, not in obedience.

Keeshah was three times my size. His razor-sharp claws were as long as my own fingers.

Question, I thought. *What does a sha'um do when the carnival comes to town?*

Answer. Anything he wants.

I knew the sha'um would never hurt me, but a wave of apprehension swept through me. Keeshah had challenged an ordinary, sensible suggestion. In spite of what he had told me, I knew *something* was wrong—but not *what*. That troubled me more than anything else. After all our close sharing, I couldn't tell, automatically, what was troubling him.

Keeshah slowed down, solving at least one problem. *All right,* he said. *Rest. But go soon?*

It was less a question than an ultimatum. I checked my convenient Gandalaran "inner awareness" and realized that dawn was only a couple of hours away.

As soon as it's light, I promised. It was far less rest than

6

Tarani or I needed, but I wasn't sure Keeshah would allow a longer delay. The uncertainty was awkward and unsettling.

Keeshah crouched down to let us step off his back. Tarani was still mostly asleep; I heard the raspy sound of shifting sand as she staggered a bit. As Keeshah moved away from us, I reached out to steady her, and she fell into my arms.

I felt a surge of protectiveness and tenderness as I held her. Protection she didn't need; we had been through too much together for me to underestimate her toughness. But the tenderness seemed to be welcome.

Tarani was taller than most Gandalaran women, her body slim and supple from years of dancing, a little thin now from the past several days of hurried travel. I stroked her headfur with my cheek. Her body tensed; she raised her head and brought her hand up to find my face in the darkness.

I pulled her more tightly against me as we kissed. I wasn't thinking of the night in Eddarta, or of the reasons I had turned away from her then. I wasn't remembering her association with Molik, or her engagement to Thymas. I wasn't even aware, consciously, of what Thymas had said just a few hours ago, right before he had left us: "She loves *you*."

I was just holding her, and it felt good. Then she moved in my arms, stepped away, tugged at my hand. It was too dark to see her face, but I had no trouble reading the invitation.

I had the same trouble accepting it as I'd faced in Eddarta.

Tarani was two women—but she didn't know that, and I couldn't bring myself to tell her.

Whatever force had snatched Ricardo Carillo's personality from the deck of a Mediterranean cruise ship had also brought Antonia Alderuccio, a sophisticated, worldly, and wealthy young woman with whom Ricardo had been talking. Antonia's personality had arrived in Gandalara four years, objective time, before I had awakened in Markasset's body.

More than the time factor was different. I had *replaced* a Gandalaran personality that had died only moments before my arrival. Tarani had been sixteen years old, and very much alive, when Antonia took up residence.

This was all deduction, based on what I knew of the disruption that had changed Tarani's life at age sixteen, and supported by one startling piece of evidence. In Eddarta, moved by passion, Tarani had spoken my *human* name, *Ricardo*. She hadn't heard the difference from *Rikardon*, hadn't noticed the absence of a final consonant, characteristic of Gandalaran names for men. The realization had hit me in a shocking flash of intuition, destroying the mood between us.

Now, as then, I struggled with the conflict. Which woman attracted me, Tarani or Antonia? Could I risk telling Tarani the truth, when doing so would expose the lie which had lain between us since we met? Tarani, like the other few Gandalarans who knew I was no longer Markasset, believed that I was a "Visitor" from the ancient past of her own world, not an absolute stranger. I couldn't discuss Antonia without introducing her to Ricardo.

Entirely aside from how she would feel about me, however, my primary question was: how would she feel about *Antonia*, the alien personality which had detected the sexual value of Tarani's illusion skills, and had guided the virginal sixteen-year-old into a profitable, but life-marking liaison with a powerful roguelord? Tarani had been well taught by Volitar to despise any means by which one person controlled the life of another. I could only think that, if she knew about Antonia's presence and subtle influences, she would feel manipulated, degraded, and furious.

Rejecting Tarani without giving her *any* reason wasn't honest, or even nice—but...

"Keeshah's restless," I said, hanging back from her tugging. "We only have a few hours to sleep—"

She stopped, and we stood silent for a moment, barely visible to one another, our hands touching in a carefully neutral manner. At last she asked: "Will it be like this all the way to Raithskar?"

I hesitated. "I don't know," I said.

She released my hand. "The answer, then, is yes," she said, impatience plain in her voice. "I do not know how it is that you can bear the continual pressure of this need, Rikardon, but I cannot. It must either be satisfied or set aside entirely. You have made that choice for us."

"I have no choice," I said lamely. "If I did..."

"Speak not of caring," she snapped, then her voice softened. "Not until this—restriction which I cannot understand has left us." An awkward silence followed. "Rest well," she said at last, and moved away from me.

The soft whisper of cloth against cloth helped me follow her movements as she settled herself in the sand and rocked back and forth to dig out a body-shaped groove. After once more fighting and controlling the impulse to join her, I pressed out my own sleeping area.

She was right; the choice was made. And I was no happier with it than she was.

I reached out to Keeshah for comfort, and found him still restless, the odd blockage still present. For the first time since I had arrived in Gandalara, I felt lonely.

2

I woke up to a sense of panic. The cloud layer above us was luminous with the spreading waves of color that marked sunrise in Gandalara, and a sleek shadow wheeled overhead. Part of my mind recognized the shadow as Lonna, the large-winged bird who was Tarani's companion, while another part rejected it as the source of the panicky feeling. That disturbance came from inside, and it wasn't entirely my own.

Keeshah! I called. *What is it? What's the matter?*

I looked around for the sha'um and saw him, several yards away, looking tense and restless. His tawny fur rippled with color and muscle as he paced beneath the reddening sky.

It was an ordinary sight—usually the sha'um was ready to travel before I was, and his impatience often made itself known to my sleeping mind and awakened me. But this was far from an ordinary morning.

For one thing, Keeshah's movement had a different character. This was no graceful, leg-stretching, wakeup kind of activity. Keeshah took only a few quick steps in any one direction before whirling to start in another. His tail whipped back and forth as he walked, now and then kicking up little puffs of sand where it lashed against the ground.

The most significant change was in the silence. There was usually a soft, growling mumbling noise, as though the huge cat were talking to himself. Often, too, through our sometimes subconscious telepathic link would flow a stream of good-natured banter of the "move it out, sleepyhead!" variety.

Both of Keeshah's voices were missing.

It scared me.

"Rikardon!"

There was urgency in Tarani's voice, and I forced my attention to focus on her. She was sitting up in the sand not ten feet from me. The big white bird had settled, wingtips crossed at the base of her tail, on Tarani's outstretched leg, and was crooning softly under Tarani's caressing hand.

"Lonna tells me that we are being followed."

"How many?" I asked, rather sharply. Keeshah's silence was omnipresent, a weight on my spirit. I had to struggle to control the panic that swelled within me—I couldn't tell whether it was Keeshah's feeling, or merely my own reaction to his oddness. "How far away are they?"

Tarani slipped into communication with the beautiful bird, using a mindlink that was only barely similar to what I shared with Keeshah. Tarani had told me that theirs was primarily an exchange of images. The bird could hold images of where to go or who to find, and remember what she saw, so that she had been useful more than once as a messenger and scout. She had also, under Tarani's direction, saved my life in Dyskornis and helped us fight off wild vineh on our trip toward Eddarta. The few seconds Tarani communed with Lonna seemed an eternity.

"Only two men," she said at last. "But there are six dralda with them, and they are barely two days behind us."

"Dralda?" I repeated, groping through Markasset's memory for the meaning of the word. I discovered that, to the young Gandalaran, it really was little more than a word. But if Markasset had never seen the creature it named, Ricardo had some association for its vague image. *Dogs,* I thought. *Wild dogs. Tarani said she formed her bond with Lonna by saving the bird from a dralda. But I've heard the word since then . . .* "Zefra!"

"What about Zefra?" Tarani asked.

"I was just remembering," I said. "The night I met Zefra in the garden, she mentioned 'Pylomel's dralda'." I smiled a little shakily, the strange unrest making it seem as if my nerve ends were remote and hard to control. "Your mother threatened to feed them my heart, if you came to harm."

She smiled back, and I could see that the thought of her mother's concern made her feel sad and tender. Then she shook her shoulders a bit—a gesture I had learned to associate with moving away from memory—and said: "Yes, she mentioned to me that the High Lord had managed to have some dralda trained for hunting. What puzzles me is—there are two men among the dralda, setting the pace for their travel, and yet they are amazingly close. How can that be?"

I puzzled over that for a moment, too. Keeshah could

11

travel three times as fast as a man—that is, the Gandalaran standard of distance was a "day", referring to the distance a man could travel in one day. Keeshah could travel a "day" in only a few hours. The measurement was based on an average, of course, but by that standard, any man-speed pursuit should be at least three days behind us, maybe four.

"If there are only two of them," I said, "that, in itself, would give them a little extra speed. Indomel must have sent them out right after we left." I didn't want to mention the prerequisite to that action. When we had left Lord Hall, Zefra had laid a compulsion on Indomel, her son and———thanks to Thymas's dagger in Pylomel's heart———the new High Lord. For Indomel to have acted so quickly, he'd have had to throw off Zefra's control. What had he done to Zefra then? "That still doesn't account for their closeness," I said. "Indomel must have picked the fastest..."

Oh, no, I thought.

"Tarani, the men—is one of them a little guy, with almost a reddish tone to his headfur?"

She nodded. "You know him?"

"Obilin," I said grimly. She looked blank for a second, then realization crossed her face.

"The High Guardsman whom Pylomel sent to claim Rassa," she said, and shuddered. "Not a pleasant man."

That's an understatement, I thought grimly.

"He's *the* High Guardsman," I said. "I had to fight him to get that place in the guard, and you can bet he's put me together with Pylomel's death. He probably begged Indomel to let him come after me."

"I see that he might be faster than other men," Tarani said, "and spurred on by his pride. But the other man—"

"Wouldn't dare *not* keep up, if you see what I mean."

She nodded thoughtfully.

"Still," I said, with a reassurance not entirely sincere, "we have a good lead, and Keeshah's speed will increase it quickly..."

Tarani stared at me as my voice trailed off, but I turned my head away from her to stare, in turn, at Keeshah.

Must go now, Keeshah had announced to me through our mindlink.

I refused to understand what he meant.

We are ready to travel, I assured him hurriedly.

Must go alone, he said. *To the Valley. Now.*

Keeshah took a few steps away from me, his head lowered, the powerful muscles of his shoulders tense to the point of stiffness.

"Rikardon?" Tarani's voice was far away, unimportant.

The Valley of the Sha'um—Keeshah's birthplace. Fear crawled in my groin, coated my tongue with bitterness. Markasset had always known that Keeshah would need to return to the Valley one day. The only sha'um who left the Valley were males. They were required, for the sake of the species, to go back and mate. Sometimes they were gone for a year or so. Sometimes—my heart stopped at the thought—sometimes they never came back from the Valley.

Let me come with you, I begged.

Keeshah whirled and stalked back toward me, impatience growling in his throat. His mane rippled up around his neck; his tail whipped up a frenzy of dust behind him. The block between his mind and mine dissolved as Keeshah reached out to me, trying to make me understand. Then it was clear that he had been hiding from me only to spare me.

I caught my breath and flinched physically at the onslaught of emotion and need. I wasn't aware of Tarani's hand on my shoulder, her voice urging and questioning. I was in the grip of an obsession, a need far stronger than anything I had ever felt before. It was more than desire—much more.

The female who hovered, faceless, odorless, at the far range of the image which called to me was only part of the need. I longed for the cool sweetness of the forest where I had been born, for freedom from the unnatural bond to the man, for communion with my own kind, and, yes, for the challenge and the passion of the female. It was all one, and calling sweetly, imperiously, irresistably—*I had to be free of the man!*

I staggered as the contact broke. For a moment I rested, rubbing my hands over my eyes to shake off the lingering touch of Keeshah's rage. Then I stepped forward, my heart aching when the big cat backed away. But I had to touch him once more. I couldn't let him go without saving one memory of his fur against my face, his muscles smooth and hard under my hand. He suffered my approach, and *endured* my arms around his neck for a moment, then shook himself and sidestepped.

Through the overwhelming tangle of emotions, I caught a light, flickering thought from him: *Can't help it. Sorry.*

13

I know, Keeshah, I told him hurting all through my body and mind. *Come back to me, if you can.*

Yes. His mindvoice was faint, fading. *Try.*

He stood only a few feet away from me, but Keeshah was already gone, his consciousness totally absorbed in the need that had claimed him.

It was a stranger I watched, a beautiful, dangerous animal, as Keeshah laid back his ears, tested the air, and ran westward—without looking back.

I was alone.

It didn't matter that Tarani was near me, speaking across the vast gulf of physical space. I saw her, felt her touch, occasionally answered her questions—though usually I didn't bother. I had a memory that she was important to me, that I cared for her. But the memory had the disreality of hallucination, the detached feeling of a dream.

It was almost as though I had been cast back to my first few hours in Gandalara, before Keeshah had touched my mind with his. Once more was I lost, confused, and *alone*, in the middle of a salty desert moving under a pale, heat-soaked sky.

In that earlier time, my fuddled mind had focused on the Great Wall as the only reasonable hope for survival, and I had put all my effort into moving toward it. The high escarpment behind Raithskar had been no more than a blue line on the horizon, probably indistinguishable from the southern "wall" of impassable mountains. Some remnant of Markasset—or his inner awareness, unrecognized then—had fixed Ricardo's attention on the important target.

In somewhat the same way, I was now getting messages from the thinking Rikardon, who seemed so separate an individual that I felt a fierce envy toward him. *He* had been Keeshah's friend. *He* had been able to think clearly, make plans, carry them out.

By contrast, *I* was able only to cling to what *he* said was important. Yet I grasped at his advice gratefully, relieved that I was spared the enormous effort of making a decision.

This time, too, I had an all-absorbing focus for my energies: the Ra'ira.

The blue jewel, enclosed in my leather belt pouch, burned in my awareness with an almost physical warmth. I couldn't distinguish the discreet elements of its importance to me, or recall the history which had brought me to this point.

I didn't remember that I had pursued the Ra'ira as if it were an ordinary, if symbolically significant, gemstone. I didn't have any conscious awareness of having discovered that it could amplify ordinary mindpower and permit direct telepathy, otherwise unknown between people. Its ancient significance, both in the benevolent formation of the Kingdom and in the malevolent abuse of the gem's power that had brought Kä into ruin, was only a vague fact.

All these were part of a single, rock-solid piece of emotional information: the Ra'ira was dangerous, and it was my job to take it back to Raithskar, where it would be safe from misuse.

I translated that directive into absolute concentration on two physical actions. One—keep the Ra'ira safe. I actually held the pouch in my hand, so that I could continually confirm my possession of the oddly shaped jewel. Two—keep moving.

I followed those directives totally. Some part of me saw the featureless sand I marched across. I was aware of a raging thirst, but it never became enough of a need to distract me from those other imperatives. I just kept walking through the heat and fine, salty dust.

It seemed obvious to me which way to go—the same way Keeshah had gone.

It could have been my loneliness pulling me in the big cat's wake. It could have been my awareness that the way to Raithskar lay through the narrow and treacherous Chizan Passages, and that the sha'um would be taking the quickest approach to Chizan. It didn't occur to me to consider that Keeshah's speed was three times mine, and that he had less need for food and water, more tolerance in general for the desert crossing.

It was part of the directive: *follow Keeshah*.

Tarani didn't agree. She pulled at me periodically, shouting words it was too much trouble to try to understand. I recognized Obilin's name, heard a word that was only vaguely familiar: *dralda*. Once Tarani tripped me, grabbed one of my feet, and dragged. Lonna was there, too, clutching at the loose fabric of my desert trousers and lifting.

I kicked out, caught Tarani in the stomach, sent her sprawling. I helped her up, said something harsh, and staggered away. I had thought that all feeling had left me, but when Tarani followed after me then, a small gladness crept into the void where emotion had been.

15

Darkness. It was only slightly cooler, but it brought relief from the eye-hurting vista of pale sand.

We rested. Tarani's humming woke me. I lay quietly for a time, listening to the melody, becoming aware of physical discomfort—hunger, thirst, a trembling weakness. Tarani's hypnotic voice promised relief, if I would yield to it. But it was nearly dawn, and the drive to be moving was on me again. Only weakness kept me still, as I summoned the energy to stand and walk.

I lay idle for so long that Tarani must have believed her mindspell had worked. She began to pry gently at the fingers that enclosed the leather pouch—and the Ra'ira.

The remote gladness I had felt in Tarani's company the day before vanished in a wave of rage. I lashed out with the hand that held the pouch; my fist caught the left side of her jaw. Tarani fell over, rolled, jumped to her feet as I staggered up. I saw, but barely noticed that she, too, was moving unsteadily, that her face looked as parched and puffy as mine felt.

"Traitor!" I thought I was yelling, but the sound I heard was a hoarse whisper. "Is this why you've stayed with me—to steal the Ra'ira for yourself?"

"Fool!" she spat back, caressing her darkening jaw with the back of her hand. "Obilin is almost on us! Can you not hear the dralda?"

Dralda. *Pylomel's dralda.* Only the barest link existed between the remembered, meaningless words and the sound I heard. The mournful coughing, drifting closer as we listened, lifted the fur along the back of my neck.

"Escape is impossible now," Tarani said. "Do you want Indomel to have the Ra'ira? Throw it away, Rikardon!" she gasped, commanding and pleading in the same breath. "Bury it in the sand!"

I struggled with confusion, watching Tarani warily as she stepped a little closer to me.

"We'd never find it again," I protested.

"It is better lost than in service to Indomel's power," she grated, and lunged to grab the pouch.

I snatched my hand back, tottering in reaction to the sudden movement. "There are no dralda," I snarled. "The sound is one of your illusions, a trick to get the Ra'ira for yourself!" I moved off, waving her away. "Stay back," I warned her.

"It is not an illusion," Tarani said, with such a tone of hopelessness that I found myself swept up in a new confusion.

"We got away from Eddarta," I said. "We brought the Ra'ira away from Gharlas and Pylomel and Indomel. We escaped. The Ra'ira is safe now," I said, with the fierceness of a child who hopes that saying a thing will make it true.

I heard the sound again, blood-stopping in its strangeness and its eagerness.

It's true, I thought, *we're still in danger. But I—I have to get the Ra'ira to Raithskar. I've been doing my best, without Keeshah. It wasn't fair that Keeshah had to leave. I've been doing all I could. Haven't I?*

They're almost here, I realized in a panic. *We'll be killed and Indomel will get the Ra'ira. I—I've failed. But it isn't my fault, it's Keeshah's. No, that's wrong, Keeshah couldn't help it. It's not Keeshah's fault. It's . . .*

"It's your fault!" I cried to Tarani, turning fear and despair into a seething rage. "You think I don't remember, but I do. We were two days ahead of them when Keeshah left, *two days*. You've been pulling at me, dragging on me, holding us back. If it weren't for you, we'd still be far ahead of them. *It's your fault!*"

I stepped up to her, my right arm poised for a swing.

She stepped back, and her sword appeared in her hand.

"The next time you strike me," she said, "will be the last time."

I stopped, stunned and surprised by the savage menace in her voice and posture.

"You have resisted everything I tried to do to save us," she said, shouting now to be heard over the noise of pursuit. "The dralda have to be following *Keeshah's* scent, and I've been trying to move us *away* from Keeshah's track. It may be too late for us," she said, "but I refuse to let your foolishness cost us the final prize.

"*Now, Lonna!*"

A streak of white flashed by me. The bird's claws raked my left hand; the pain startled me into dropping the pouch. Lonna banked a sharp turn and dipped close to the ground to grab up the piece of leather and its contents.

"No!" I shouted and dived. My hands closed around the pouch just as Lonna grabbed it. "Protecting the Ra'ira is *my* job!"

The bird screeched; Tarani shouted; the eerie call of the

dralda drew nearer. I clung desperately to the piece of leather while the bird's wings beat blindingly against my face and her claws pulled at pouch and hands indiscriminately. I ignored the pain of the scratches, the sting as my bloody hands were pressed into the salty sand.

"Enough, Lonna," Tarani said at last, and there was silence. The beating wings stilled as Lonna paused and looked questioningly at the girl. The bird's full weight rested on my outstretched hands, clenched together around the scarred pouch. Lonna rested with her wings folded, but not quite relaxed, her beak parted. She was panting from the effort of our struggle. Tarani knelt by us and smoothed the feathers on the bird's breast.

"Why is it so quiet?" I panted.

Tarani merely looked at me, then coaxed the bird to a perch on her outstretched arm. She stood up. "There is nothing more you can do, Lonna," she said. "Go quickly, and be safe."

The bird launched herself, circled us once screeching her frustration, then flew straight up, her white body disappearing against the clouds.

"Why is it so quiet?" I asked again, sitting up.

All of the desert area of Gandalara seemed flat. Its hilly contours made themselves noticed in two ways—first, by the strain in your legs as you walked up and down the mounded sand; and second, when something or someone, hidden by the gentle hills, appeared as if from out of nowhere.

The dralda appeared now, too excited over the end of the hunt even to howl.

3

The dralda were dog-like in the same sense that the sha'um were cat-like—they shared qualities I identified with dogs, but there were differences from the animals Ricardo had known. As with every other mammalian creature in Gandalara, the canine teeth of the dralda were longer and wider than those of their counterparts in Ricardo's world—sharp tusks rather than teeth. This, and a swift impression of the high-shouldered shape of a hyena combined with the size of a great dane, were all I could tell about the animals before one slammed into me, knocking me backward with breath-killing force.

I threw up my arms to protect my face, but I needn't have bothered. The dog merely stood with its forepaws pressing into my chest. I could clearly feel each of eight sharp claws pricking into my skin. Its head loomed over my face, its lips drawn back. A soft growl vibrated through its paws.

I turned my head cautiously. Tarani was pinned underneath the massive body of another dralda. The remaining animals circled us, seemingly frustrated that their prey had already been claimed. Then, from beyond Tarani, one lowered its nose to the sand and snuffled. It lifted its head and howled; the other uncommitted dralda echoed the cry, and the whole pack of them started off running.

She was right, I realized, through my daze. *They were following Keeshah—until they were close enough to catch our scent directly. And if Tarani was right about that? . . .*

What's been happening to me? What have I done to us?

The long, stout muzzle of the beast turned in the direction the others had gone. The dralda trembled with the conflict—join the hunt, or protect the catch? I held my breath, grasping at the hope that the hunt would win.

Two men topped the dune, one panting heavily, the larger one lurching, clutching his side, groaning with the need for

19

air. Obilin looked down at us, and smiled. The other man dropped to his knees, gasping.

The small man came down the shallow angle of the dune to stand above me. He glanced at Tarani, half-blocked from his view by the body of the dralda that pinned her. "The girl is here," he said. "She's the one the High Lord wants. Her, and this." He leaned over and tried to take the pouch; I jerked it away from him; the dralda growled; Obilin drew his sword and put its point to my throat. "Would you like to live a few minutes longer?" he asked.

I gave him the pouch. He straightened up, and I heard a soft moan from Tarani. It echoed accusingly through my mind.

My fault. Mine.

"We have what Indomel wants," Obilin said again. He pressed the sword's point downward only slightly. I felt a pricking, and a warm trickle of blood. "And *I* have what *I* want."

He pulled away the sword and turned to the other man. "The third one abandoned them, obviously," Obilin said. "He can't be far ahead, but he's not important. Go after them, Sharam," he ordered, waving in the direction the dralda had gone. "Call them back."

Obilin didn't get any argument. The man forced himself to his feet and obeyed, traveling in an uncontrolled, bone-jarring trot.

Obilin walked around me toward Tarani, laughing softly. Fine particles of sand had settled into his reddish-blond head fur, graying it into a nearly white frame for his small, well-defined features. Obilin's skin was the same color as mine— about the shade a human Caucasian achieves after weeks of effort at tanning. The light color of his dusted hair provided a contrast that made his good looks even more striking. I had seen enough of him in Eddarta to know he was proud of his looks and made a deliberate effort to keep his body finely toned.

I saw the proof, now, of his physical condition. His breathing was nearly normal again.

"This is working out perfectly," Obilin was saying. "When that fool catches his animals, he'll collapse for a few hours. Since we're at least two days ahead of our supply caravan, that gives us some time alone at last, my lovely Rassa—"

He had moved to a place from which he could see Tarani's face clearly, and now he flinched back in shock.

"Tarani!" he said.

Tarani, too, jumped in surprise. The dralda, paws on Tarani's shoulder and stomach, growled softly. "How—how do you know me?" she asked.

Obilin didn't answer her. He slapped his forehead with his free hand—he still held his sword—and exclaimed, laughing: "By the Last King, I should have guessed! Rassa's reappearance, when all the gossip said that she and her father had fled from the former High Lord's romantic interest. Zefra, that old fraud—do you know, she actually had me believing that *she* had forced me to deliver that false message to Pylomel? And if those weren't clues enough—the *bird!*" He shouted with laughter. "I *thought* that bird looked familiar, but I still didn't put it all together until I saw your face." He stopped laughing. "And a lovely face it is," he added softly.

He dropped the point of his sword to Tarani's cheek; I saw her eyes, still open, staring up at the little man. The swordpoint traced a path along Tarani's jaw, seemed to linger forever at the softest point of her throat, then finally moved down her chest and pressed down the woven fabric of her tunic, outlining the shape of her breast.

His breathing had quickened again.

"Ah, lovely Tarani," he breathed. "I confess that I never dreamed that this moment might come. I am even more grateful, now, that we have these private moments. Before the others arrive you shall do for me what you did, so beautifully, for Molik."

Tarani and I gasped simultaneously. Tarani hated that name, hated the memory of her service to the roguelord. She—with Antonia's hidden guidance, I was sure—had fulfilled Molik's sexual fantasies with her body and her mindpower, in exchange for something she wanted very badly—a traveling show, in which her power of illusion and her dancing provided decent, innocent entertainment. Molik was dead now, but Obilin had rekindled that terrible memory. More horribly, he planned to make her re-live it.

Suddenly, the lingering confusion cleared from my mind. *I got us into this*, I was thinking. *I got Tarani into this. We may get killed, but, by God, she won't suffer through that again!*

"You touch her, Obilin," I said, my voice dry and raspy, "and you're a dead man."

Tarani's head snapped toward me, her face betraying recognition of the change in me. Obilin looked around, too, surprised by my outburst, but obviously unworried.

Tarani grabbed the neckfur of her dralda and twisted on the ground, shoving the dog against Obilin's legs. I swung my clenched hands hard at the side of my dralda's head. It flinched away; before it could regain its balance, I was out from under it, on my feet, the weight of the steel sword welcome in my bloody hands. Desperation had restored some of the strength leeched out by the desert. Tarani was up, too, the sword she had dropped held out in front of her.

Obilin backed cautiously, keeping us both in sight. His eyes narrowed when he saw my sword, and he smiled his slick, offensive smile.

"Well, well," he said. "What's this, another disguise? The humble, if troublesome, mercenary Lakad turns into a rich prize!" He made a mock bow, keeping his eyes up. "This is indeed an honor, Rikardon. And I sympathize with your feelings for the lady. Unfortunately, that does make you a rival, doesn't it?" He pointed his free arm at me. "Tass. Mara. Attack!"

The dralda, who had kept their distance from the swords, bunched their muscles and aimed themselves at me. I braced myself to meet their charge, but suddenly they backed away, whining and whipping their heads from side to side as if in pain.

"They will not obey you, Obilin," Tarani said, drawing his attention toward her. "Your name meant nothing to me, and I did not recognize you dressed to serve a different master," she said, referring, I supposed, to the green uniform of the High Guard. "But when you spoke of Molik—I remember you now, salt-scum. You are the source of the Living Death. You stole slaves and sold them all over again to Molik, to die in his service."

Obilin was retreating from the girl's tall, crouching form. Tarani's fury was palpable, fascinating. She may have been using her mindpower to keep Obilin's attention fixed on her—because he was backing straight toward me. I lifted my sword and brought it down hilt-first with all my strength.

But Obilin had his own kind of power, drawn from years of fighting. Suspicion surfaced, and at the last possible moment, he twisted around. The hilt of my sword only grazed his shoulder. Instead of attacking me, he dropped his sword,

22

threw himself into a backward somersault, and came up on his hands. He bucked a double kick into Tarani's chest.

The girl went down like a stone, the wind knocked out of her. Obilin leaped over to her, swung a backhand blow, and she was out cold.

I was on my way to help her when both dralda hurled themselves at me. I braced myself against their weight and slashed out with my sword. One fell back with a useless front leg, but the other had its teeth in my arm and was dragging me around in a circle as it dodged my sword.

The pain in my arm was nothing compared to the pain in my mind. *Damn it, this is all my fault*, I accused myself again. *If I hadn't been so damned sorry for myself when Keeshah left, if I'd paid attention to my responsibility to Tarani and the Ra'ira...unnhh...*

Something hard hit the base of my skull, and everything went black.

Misery, anguish, remorse—none of those words can describe the way I felt when I woke up with pain shooting up my arm, an ache throbbing in my head, and guilt hovering in my mind like a thundercloud. I reached out to Keeshah for comfort...

Add loneliness.

I opened my eyes to see Obilin standing nearby, examining Rika, turning it so the sharp, steel blade winked brightness at me...

Add hatred.

Tarani's face came into view. Even with her dark headfur gray with sand and her cheek swelling from Obilin's blow, she was beautiful.

"I'm sorry," I said.

Obilin turned at the sound of my voice. "Awake? Good." He put Rika through his own baldric and came toward us, tossing and catching the leather pouch. "Perhaps one of you would like to tell me what's in this little package?"

"Look for yourself," I said wearily.

"I'm afraid that's impossible," he replied. He stopped beside me, facing Tarani. "You see, the High Lord gave me very specific orders. He wanted 'the woman' alive, and 'the pouch' unopened."

"Your loyalty is commendable," I said. "Flexible, too. How long had Pylomel been dead before you accepted those orders from Indomel? One hour? Two?"

"On that score," he said, kneeling beside me, "you are very wrong, my friend. Indomel has had my loyalty for quite a while. It suited him to have me serve Pylomel."

"I suppose you had his permission to sell slaves into the Living Death?" I asked, repressing a shudder.

The Living Death was an assassin group, dying men and women brought away from the copper mines and given a short life of luxury in exchange for assassination and suicide. I had faced two of them, and it wasn't an experience I wanted to repeat.

"I take something of little value," Obilin said with a shrug. "If he knew, Indomel would probably compliment my enterprise—before he had me killed, of course." He laughed. "Aren't you wondering," he said, after a moment, "why you're still alive?"

"You tell me," I said. I was having a hard time finding the energy to talk. Obilin had the Ra'ira, and Indomel would have it soon. Keeshah was gone. I wanted to slip away from it all, drift into a sleep from which I'd never bother to waken.

Only one thing kept me from doing it. Tarani's hands were busy with Obilin's water pouch, cleaning and dressing the wounds on my hands and arm. Her touch was a reminder that it wasn't just *my* life I'd be throwing away.

She might be better off on her own; I argued with myself. Just then, Tarani moved slightly, pressing her knee into my side. I looked up at her, and she managed a smile.

Obilin noticed the look we exchanged. "Yes, you're right, the lady is partially responsible for your well being. We determined, after several, ah, contests, that she can't control me and the dralda at the same time, so we struck a bargain— I let you live in exchange for her promise not to use her power on me.

"What she doesn't know, however," he added, standing up to pace around us, "is that you're far more valuable to me alive than dead." He laughed again. "I had no intention of killing you in the first place."

"Then that means the bargain is off, doesn't it?" I said. "He's talking about the reward, Tarani. Worfit, remember?"

She nodded. "The roguelord in Raithskar. You thought he had sent the Living Death after you, when it had been Gharlas who had wanted Dharak dead."

The sound of Dharak's name brought a flood of memories

24

of him, of Thymas his son, of Thagorn. *We could use a troop of Sharith about now*, I thought. *Just Thymas and his sha'um, Ronar, would help.* I winced from the pain of a wound greater than the ones Tarani was treating. *Hell, all I need is Keeshah. God, I wish he were still with us.*

"Worfit is no longer in Raithskar," Obilin said. "He has taken over Molik's operation in Chizan—every inch of it. He does hate you, Rikardon," he said, pointing the pouch at me. "That's a story I'd like to hear someday. When I first heard about the reward, it was ten thousand zaks for you and the sword, dead or alive. After you were spotted in Dyskornis, the ante went up—ten thousand for the sword, and ten thousand more for you—*alive*."

He knelt again, and brought his face close to mine. He was, indeed, a handsome man if you could look only at his body. But his personality was too visible. He wore his nastiness like a top hat.

"It's not the money I want, Rikardon," he said. "You're going to be a goodwill gift to the new master of Chizan's rogueworld. I'll expect the money, too, but I'll trade half of it for the privilege of watching whatever Worfit has planned for you. It should start our personal dealings off well."

"You haven't met him?" I asked.

"Not yet," he said. "Though we are already doing business. Is there something I should know about him?"

"Nothing you don't already know about yourself," I said. "You're a perfect pair."

Obilin laughed again and rocked back on his heels. His laugh stopped abruptly. "It has just occurred to me that neither of you seem surprised about Worfit's new position. Could it be that you already knew Molik was dead?" We just stared at him. "A-huh."

He stood up. "Well, the bargain *isn't* off," he said. "If I had to choose either Worfit or Indomel to offend, it would be Worfit, I assure you. So you and the lady are coming back to Eddarta with me. After I turn her and this," he waved the pouch, "whatever it is, over to Indomel, I plan to take an inspection tour of the mines—except that Rikardon and I will really go west to Chizan, exactly as I did the first time I saw you, lovely lady." He bowed slightly.

"However, keep in mind that I have the sword, which is worth as much as the man. Your power doesn't frighten me, now that I have seen its limits. If you use it to try to escape, I promise you *he will die*."

"It is a bargain, Obilin," she said.

"No!" I started to protest, until I looked into Tarani's eyes. Anger and contempt for Obilin burned there, and determination and—shattering what little pride remained to me—protectiveness. The fierceness of that look, hidden from Obilin, was such a contrast to the meekness of her voice that I was stunned into silence.

"I'm almost sorry," Obilin said, "that your feelings for *him* make the bargain practical." He tossed up the pouch, caught it again. "Tarani."

We both looked at him.

"There is something else I want. You know that. Is there nothing you will take in trade?"

Tarani started to shake. I felt the trembling in her hands, in the knee which still pressed against me, in the sand which lay between us. I saw the thought in her face: *Could she get the Ra'ira back that way?* I was watching when the answer hit, too: *No. Don't trust Obilin*. Through it all, even greater once the answer was clear, I could sense her rage that he should even ask.

Her stage training showed. Face and voice were composed, hiding the seething fury, as she said: "There is nothing I want that much."

I had been so fascinated by her reaction that I'd ignored my own. Now I discovered I was shaking inside, too. And there was nothing to be gained by hiding *my* feelings.

"Obilin."

He turned his gaze to me, and his face went pale.

"*Don't mention it again*," I said.

He seemed about to say something, then he changed his mind. He backed away and sat down near the two dralda, who lay panting nearby.

"Don't stay for my sake," I whispered to Tarani.

She had finished bandaging my arm and washing the less severe scratches on my hand. She lifted my head and helped me take a sip of water—enough to cool my mouth, not enough to choke my swollen throat.

"Where would I go?" she whispered back.

4

The other dralda and their handler, Sharam, returned within the hour. When he had rested, Sharam entered into a whispered discussion with Obilin. It quickly turned into an argument, and ended with Sharam shrugging and moving off toward his animals. Obilin came over to us.

"There is another part of the bargain," he said, his voice allowing no disagreement. "Sharam tells me his dralda think they have been chasing a sha'um. I have never seen one, but I know enough to be sure that if one *had* been with you, he would *still* be with you."

I tried not to let my face show how much that statement hurt me, and I worked on another puzzle.

If Obilin knows about the sword, why doesn't he know about Keeshah, too? Of course—he's heard about me the way every rogueworld district in Gandalara has heard about me—from Worfit, who wouldn't give out information which would discourage anybody from coming after me. Worfit has simply neglected to mention that his target usually travels in the company of a very big, very protective cat.

"I conclude, therefore," Obilin said, "that the sha'um was an invention of the lady's, to confuse the people who saw you leave Eddarta, and to mislead the dralda. Tarani, you will not use your power *at all* on the journey back to Eddarta. On *anyone*. Understood?"

Tarani nodded. Obilin turned away, and from that moment on treated us as indifferently as he might treat slaves.

We rested the remainder of the day and the night, and moved slowly eastward on the next day. Toward dusk, we met the supply caravan which had followed Obilin from Eddarta, and my thirst and hunger were satisfied for the first time in what seemed like years. The journey became routine after that, physically easier as Tarani's tending helped my body heal, but mentally burdensome with every step we took closer to Eddarta.

27

Though neither Tarani nor I dared mention the Ra'ira, I was sure that it was as much on her mind as it was on mine. Obilin had set up the marching order so that we were together—more from unwillingness to bother any of his men with my care than out of consideration for us—and both of us did a lot of staring at the leather pouch swinging at Obilin's belt. It was as though the blue jewel sent out a glow visible only to us.

It was usually when the group stopped for the night or assembled to begin the day's march that she and I found ourselves more alone than at other times of the day. On the morning of the fourth day, I broke what had become a weighty silence between us.

"In the desert," I whispered to her, "it made sense to stay with Obilin's group. But we're coming into farmland. You could survive here. You know how much a promise *from* Obilin would be worth—you don't need to keep a promise *to* him . . . especially not on my account."

She had taken off her knee-high boots to empty and dust them, and was in the process of putting them back on. She waited until both boots were on, then stood up to face me. "It is not my promise to Obilin that keeps me here," she said quietly, then looked at me directly. "Nor is it you—except that escape will be more likely to succeed if we are together."

"Succeed?" I said. "Like this one did, while we were together?"

Her eyes narrowed. "Did you know Keeshah would leave us?" she asked.

I had to swallow a huge lump to open my throat for speech. The absence of the big cat still hurt—all the time, every minute. Underlying every thought was a continuous fretting: would Keeshah come out of the Valley?

"No," I managed to say.

"Then you can hardly take credit for our capture," she said.

The other men in the group had finished assembling their backpacks and were gathering closer. Obilin had a look of impatience I had learned to recognize as ready-to-move-out, and was walking toward us. As always, when he saw Tarani, a new expression crossed his face—sort of a soft amusement that spoke of secret plans.

Tarani turned her back to him so he couldn't see her face and whispered: "My promise lasts only until we reach Eddarta.

28

Be ready." Then she reached out and pressed my shoulder with her hand.

Except for her tending to my wounds, it was the first gentle touch we had shared since Keeshah had left. I was moved by her forgivingness and encouragement, but there was no time for words. I pressed my hand over hers and, for that one moment, we were together again.

Obilin hadn't missed the gesture or its significance. There was no change in his outward manner—that is, his orders to the group were no less gruff—but there was a special look for me when I came into his visual range.

Our entry into Eddarta wouldn't have rivaled Caesar's return from Gaul. Dusty and tired, the troop of us dragged our way closer to the sprawling city that was the domain—but not the dwelling place—of the Lords of Eddarta. The seven Lords and their families lived in a second city that crowned a rise of land above Eddarta. "Lord City" was joined to what I thought of as "lower Eddarta" by a wide, paved road and a rushing line of water that was one of the larger branches of the Tashal River.

Sight of the shining river stirred me in many ways. First and most basic, Markasset came from a culture which was reminded daily that the difference between living and dying— for a man or for a city—was the presence of water. Beyond that, seeing this and the other branches of the Tashal tumble their way down from a point so high on the River Wall that the cloud cover obscured it reminded Markasset of the Skarkel Falls and River that shimmered behind Raithskar. If Markasset's personality, as well as his memories, had been present in this body, he would have been homesick.

I felt the tug of longing, too—but for a different "where". It was impossible not to look at the river and see three people clinging to a cluster of rope-tied reeds . . . to remember the sight and smell of torches burning in the still night air . . . to sense, rather than see, the hulking outlines of the sha'um against the wavering light . . . the gold-filled belt . . .

(I put my hands to my waist, surprised by the memory. The belt was there, the gold pieces securely hidden within the leather. *How could I have forgotten it?* I wondered. *It's a fortune. Could I have used it with Obilin—no*, I answered myself immediately, and felt a quick thrill of hope. *But it may yet come in handy*, I thought, and slipped back into the memory.)

The gold-filled belt arching toward the shore trailing a rope . . . the cat's snatching at it, pulling . . . joy spilling from Keeshah, even while he complained.

Wet, he had said, laughing in his mind while his body carried us away from Eddarta.

Keeshah! I called, and touched only emptiness.

Oh, God, Keeshah . . .

Tarani touched my arm, and I jumped. The sudden movement set off the restless dralda, leashed two to a man behind us, and their howling upset every vlek within a range of two hundred feet. Those traveling with us or in our direction weren't much of a problem, since the people leading them had allowed us plenty of distance. But there was a group coming west with twenty or so of the stupid pack animals strung out in a long line. The vlek handlers had been doing all right, so long as their goat-size charges had been merely suspicious of the passing dralda. Pandemonium broke loose when the dralda started making noise.

I could well understand the vleks being terrified—*I* felt threatened by the fur-lifting sound the dralda made. But that didn't make the sudden confusion and noise any easier to bear—vleks bawling, dralda howling, men cursing. I felt as if I could crawl right out of my skin.

The men were doing their best to hold the dralda, but apparently it was only the handler who could calm them into silence. That took a hand touch and some intense concentration, and wasn't guaranteed, as the first one proved, just as the handler reached number four. Six dralda, one man, *big* noise.

The caravan people were yelling at the guards who held the dralda; the guards were yelling at the handler, who was yelling back in frustration. I sympathized with his situation; I knew he had to be calm in order to soothe the animals, and nobody would leave him alone long enough to do his job. Obilin finally got into the act, shouting his own people into silence.

I realized that Tarani and I were alone.

"Now," I whispered, grabbing her arm and edging her toward the caravan. "Get away while you can."

She pulled her arm out of my grip. "Without the Ra'ira?"

"You said Eddarta," I reminded her. "This is Eddarta. Now go."

Once more I tried to push her into the confusion of the caravan. She pushed back—so hard that I staggered.

I stared at her, trying to understand. We both knew that her ability to disguise herself through illusion would see her safe from the city, at least. She had as much as told me that she wasn't hanging around on my account—that is, not in order to protect me, or out of loyalty. That left only what she had said: the Ra'ira. I started to tell her that I'd get the Ra'ira and meet her somewhere, but then I wondered. We had been a team of three when we escaped with it the first time, and Tarani's skills had been an essential part of that team. Could I do it alone?

It's obvious why she won't go, I thought painfully. *She's accepted the duty to return the Ra'ira to Raithskar. I've flat proved that I can't be counted on. She won't leave until that stone is safe in her own two hands.*

Tarani watched me think about it, and sensed when I'd completed the logic. Then she pressed my arm with her hands and whispered: "You see, we are both needed for this task."

Kind of you to include me, I thought bitterly. I knew full well how irrational it was to resent her consideration of my feelings, but I couldn't help it. *You'll be the one to do it, if anyone can. Providing either one of us lives past seeing Indomel.*

Our moment of aloneness ended abruptly as Obilin charged over to us. "Help the handler calm them," he ordered Tarani. A dagger, hidden from everyone but me, pressed against her ribs when she tried to move past Obilin toward the dralda.

"You see how he does it," she protested. "A touch is necessary—"

"A touch wasn't necessary when I ordered one to attack you," he reminded her. "I won't have you display your power, but neither will I waste any more time with this nonsense. Silence the dralda!"

"But the handler is soothing—what I did was different, a command. It—I hate doing that—enough of it will make them useless to the handler—they will turn on him—"

"Do it!" Obilin ordered.

Tarani clenched her teeth, closed her eyes . . . and the dralda were quiet.

I looked from the animals, who were shuffling their feet and shaking their heads slightly, as though they had been

31

stunned, to Tarani, whose face had gone past its normal paleness into a sick pallor. The skin had shrunk back against her skull, hollowing the areas beneath her fine cheekbones.

She opened her eyes and reached for my hand; I held it while the trembling passed. As always, Obilin showed enjoyment of her discomfort, disapproval (if not actual jealousy) of our closeness, and anticipation of a final confrontation with me.

By now, I thought, *he ought to be able to read me well enough to see how much I'm looking forward to it, too.*

When Tarani had made her move, the dralda had voiced, in chorus, an upswinging whine of surprise. The noise itself had been bad enough; when it ended so abruptly, everybody— man and beast—became quietly alert. I guess even the vleks figured that it wouldn't be wise to attract the attention of anything that could scare a dralda.

So when the return column resumed its journey toward Eddarta, the only sounds were Obilin's clipped orders and the whisper of leather-shod feet against the hard-packed dirt of the roadway. The silence was positively eerie, and we carried it with us long enough for me to catch the content of what was whispered among three men who passed us leading a pack vlek loaded with baked goods.

"Obilin!" one said in surprise. "Who is that with him?"

"In his proclamation, Indomel said that Obilin had gone after the intruders..."

"Intruders my left tusk," the other snorted. "That dralda whelp killed his father himself, I say!"

"Sssh!" the third one cautioned. "Speak softly of the High Lord! And anyway—doesn't this prove that he was telling the truth? There *were* intruders."

"Those can't be the ones, though!" the first man protested. "They had sha'um."

The group had my full attention then, but they were moving further away, and I had to strain to catch even snips of the rest of their conversation:

"...drank too much faen..."

"...other people..."

"All of them crazy..."

"...too dark to see the people clearly..."

"...there *were* sha'um, I tell you!"

Laughter and protestations, all in suppressed voices, faded as we left the group behind us.

32

The conversation had given me two important pieces of information.

First, lower Eddarta's understanding of what happened that night had to be varied and tenuous, based as it was on a blend of official statement, rumor, and skepticism.

Second, I wouldn't call Indomel beloved of his people. Even the two who had defended him seemed more concerned with whether he had been truthful than whether he had suffered any grief over his father's death.

Maybe they know him pretty well already, I thought. *Certainly the "change of command" doesn't seem to have affected them much.* I sighed. *But, then, it wouldn't. After all, it's part of the system. People come and go, but the High Lord has had his place in this society for centuries. They accept him in the same way they seem to have accepted slavery—they don't worry about it unless it involves them directly.*

That brought to mind a topic I had been avoiding. *Slavery*, I thought. *I wonder if that's what Indomel has planned for us?*

We were in the city proper by this time, and Obilin released his grip on Tarani's arm and moved down the line, tightening the formation to make the marching group less an obstacle to other pedestrians. Whispers followed along behind us—as did a ragtag group of kids, until Obilin barked at them.

I reached for Tarani's hand. She returned my grip, and even managed a quick smile. "I fear for Zefra," she whispered.

The thought had crossed my mind, too. It was obvious that Indomel knew the Ra'ira still in Eddarta was a phony. What had that discovery done to Tarani's mother, whose mindpower had been boosted by her confidence that the glass bauble would give her extra strength? When we had left Eddarta, Zefra had revealed her long-hidden mindgift, had succeeded in dominating Indomel, if only temporarily.

"Indomel doesn't strike me as the forgiving kind," I said, knowing it wasn't a comforting thought for Tarani. "But he's not stupid, either. Did you hear those men a little ways back? The Eddartans are already wondering if he's behind his *father's* death. He wouldn't dare take any steps toward his *mother*—it would be like admitting he killed Pylomel, too. I doubt if Zefra is much worse off than she was before."

Except, I thought, *that her "edge" is gone—she's revealed the strength of her mindgift to Indomel, and he'll guard against it. She's truly helpless now.*

And are we any better off? I wondered. Apprehension closed in around my chest, weighing it down so that it was hard to breathe. *Tarani talks about escaping as if it were already done. But Indomel knows her power, too, and will take precautions. As for me—I don't have Keeshah, and I don't have Rika.*

Obilin has Rika. Sharam was too tired to notice that Obilin had a different sword, and when the others arrived, Obilin hid my sword in one of the packs.

We do have information, I remembered, thinking of Obilin's involvement with Molik and Worfit, and his possession of what amounted to one of the greatest treasures in Gandalara. Then the hope of bargaining with that information died. *And Indomel has the means to get any information we have—the Ra'ira.*

I fought back my despair to return Tarani's hand-squeeze. The column had spruced itself up and picked up the pace. We were beginning the long climb to Lord City. Obilin came up on the other side of Tarani and cupped his hand protectively, possessively around her elbow.

Obilin won't tell Indomel Tarani's history, I thought. *He hasn't given up wanting her for himself.*

5

The small troop marched up the hill and through the arched gateway that separated the Lords of Eddarta from the society which supported them. I expected that we would be taken directly to Lord Hall, the octagonal building which commanded the center of attention immediately on entering Lord City. I suppose I was remembering the old Western movies of Ricardo's world, and the mock trials that were set up for "hoss thieves and russlers". I think I expected Indomel to be eager to gloat over his triumph. I know I just wanted it to be settled as fast as possible.

But my expectations and the High Lord's plans had little in common. Tarani and I were led along the entry path which approached Lord Hall. Instead of going in, we were taken around the periphery of the hall, under the continuous portico, to the covered walkway which led to the dwelling section assigned to the Harthim family.

I should have expected this, I thought, as we moved along the stone-laid walk. *Indomel will treat this as a personal score, rather than take a chance of exposing Tarani's power to other members of the Council.*

When the guards had passed into the Harthim entry, which was formed by the sides of buildings, there was a perceptible change in mood. The doorways opening from the entry led into the living quarters of the High Guard or to sentry stations. Either way, it felt like home to these guys, and I found my own mood lightening with theirs. Ever since our capture—hell, since Keeshah had left me—I had felt suspended, drifting, unable to anchor myself. Now, at least, there would be an end to that sense of disassociation. Once I learned what Indomel's plans were, I could begin to figure out how to defeat them.

I still had some notion that Tarani and I would be dragged into a courtroom-style audience with Indomel; he would gloat and preen and pronounce sentence; then we would either be

35

killed (*resolution of an unsatisfactory sort*, I thought) or left alone to plot our escape. I was eager to find out which, to get this first step over with.

Obilin halted the column and waved the men with dralda off in the direction of the garden where I had first met Zefra. The handler was wearing a frown of concentration as the men grinned and tugged hard on the leashes of their animals. It came as no surprise that they would be glad to be rid of the beasts. But the dralda followed sullenly, dragging back against the pressure of the leashes. I glanced at Tarani, but her face was a perfectly composed mask. She had said that using her power on the dralda could produce some side effects. But what did I know about dralda? This could be their normal, "What fun, it's back to captivity!" reaction.

Obilin still had hold of Tarani's arm. He waved again, and two of the guards moved in on me and started to "usher" me out of the entryway.

I dug in my heels and brought the guards up short.

"We're together, Obilin. You can't split us up like this!" I said.

Obilin only laughed, and the guards pulled at me again.

I drove the elbow of my good arm into one man's midriff, then swung the same fist at the other guy's chin. A lot of frustration found release in those simple movements. That, combined with the men's fatigue, sent them down for the count.

I stepped toward Obilin, but he had his sword out, and we both knew he really wanted me to advance against him.

"No," Tarani cried, and started toward me. Obilin's hand on her wrist pulled her back, leaving one of her arms extended in my direction. There was pleading in her voice as she said: "There is no purpose in this. I will be safe, and so shall you." She lowered her eyes, and a transformation took place.

I had already surmised that some of the discussion our passing had stirred in Eddarta had centered around Tarani. Her physical resemblance to the Lords was startling. That's not to say that no lower Eddartans had her unusual height or smooth black headfur or delicate and graceful facial planes. I had seen several individuals with similar physical characteristics, though they were more rare than I would have expected, assuming the natural passions and power of the Lords and what little I knew of genetics.

But Tarani had something no mere combination of genes could create: style. Perhaps it was her years of cultivating a stage presence. It could have been an imitation of Zefra, who knew thoroughly the subtle uses of power. Whatever the source of the change, it was visible and effective. Tarani turned back to Obilin and the little man stepped backward in surprise. He looked around quickly, and paled slightly when he saw that we were, for this passing moment, alone.

"By birth," Tarani said, "I am the natural daughter of Zefra and Pylomel."

"Indomel's *sister?*" Obilin breathed. "No wonder he was so anxious to have you brought back here."

"Indomel's *elder* sister," Tarani corrected, and waited for the significance of that statement to penetrate Obilin's thinking. "I see you understand that there is no affection between me and the present High Lord," Tarani said, with the slightest extra emphasis on the word *present*. "Understand, also, that I am not an ordinary prisoner. *Rikardon is not to be harmed.*"

Obilin's thin face flickered with plots and calculation, but in the end he seemed to decide that Tarani had won this round. He smiled sardonically.

"You have my word," he said softly, "that *as far as it lies within my power*, your friend will be cared for well. As for you—" He shrugged. "—I expect you will see to your own safety."

He called for two more guards, and didn't relax his defensive stance until they each had one of my arms.

These men were fresh and strong, and the effort of clobbering the other two had drained the last of my strength. The one I had elbowed was getting his breath back. He stood up and gave me a look so nasty that my gut muscles tightened in anticipation of his blow.

"Give him one of the smaller rooms," Obilin ordered. "Two men will be posted at his door in four-hour shifts—you two take the first shift. He is not to be talked to or allowed to leave his quarters. But neither is he to be injured. Clear?"

The two new guards nodded. The third one checked his fist in mid-swing.

"Clear?" Obilin repeated. The third one nodded and stepped back, obviously unhappy. "Tend to Mossan, then get some rest. Tell the others who were with us that they have three days off."

He turned to Tarani as Mossan was fireman-carried into the

37

barracks area. "Will these arrangements be suitable?" he asked, with just a touch of sarcasm.

"Yes, they will do for now," Tarani said as she crossed the few paces between us, this time shaking off Obilin's restraining hand. She put her hands on my chest, and her touch was oddly comforting. "We will meet again soon," she whispered and, right there in front of God and everybody, kissed me.

She went with Obilin, then, and the memory of her kiss was made sweeter by his parting look.

That's another round you've lost, Obilin, I thought as I was led to my "quarters".

The room I was led to was just like the one in which Willon had installed me, when I had hired into the High Guard as a mercenary named Lakad. One wall was covered with pegs and lashed-reed shelves for my nonexistent wardrobe. There was a small table and a couple of chairs, and a fluffy pallet for sleeping. This room had two features the other one had lacked, however.

Sturdy shutters covered the window. Small sliding panels had been arranged to allow light and air to flow through latticed reeds. The shutters were braced from the outside, making the shutters not much less effective at containment than the stone walls around the window.

One of the guards returned with the other new item: the Gandalaran equivalent of a chamberpot.

I had a feeling I was in for a long, dreary wait, and I wasn't disappointed. I had always believed that it's impossible for a thinking person to be bored, that even in enforced physical idleness, one's mind could be active. The trouble with that theory is that certain mental "activity" can be much worse than boredom.

There were two natural directions for my mind to turn: Tarani and Keeshah. Was one all right? Would the other come back?

I had been installed in my "cell" close to dusk. When I watched the red light of dawn creep in its latticed pattern across my unused pallet, I realized that I was hurting everybody by worrying. One more day of concentrated anxiety and I'd be so physically drained as to be useless to Tarani in any attempt to escape.

So I resolved *not* to think about them any more. (Except that I couldn't stop reaching out for Keeshah each time I lay down to sleep. The pain of finding emptiness never diminished.) And boy, was I bored.

The first couple of days were okay. I set up a disciplined calisthenics program to counteract my restlessness. I explored every inch of the room, looking for something to use in aid of escaping. I channeled my thinking toward my favorite unsolvable riddle: where, how, and why?

Where was Gandalara? Its physical features and its inhabitants were both like and unlike those of Ricardo's Earth; the coincidence tantalized me and the impossibility of a definite answer frustrated me.

How did Ricardo's personality wind up in Markasset's body?

There was more than one "why". Why was I here? Why Markasset's body? Why me at all?

I knew the Ra'ira was bound up in the answer to that third part of the riddle. I doubt that anyone but Tarani and me could have defeated Gharlas, because of our individually unique human/Gandalaran minds. Gharlas had planned domination over all of Gandalara, but he would have produced only strife and the eventual destruction of a centuries-old civilization.

But, with Thymas's help, we had defeated Gharlas; the man was dead and no further danger to us or Gandalara. But was the Ra'ira safely back in Raithskar? No. Was that our final purpose—to get that blasted, beautiful gem to safety? It seemed logical. But, then, I had been logical twice before: first when I deduced that my Gandalaran obligation was to prove the innocence of Markasset's father, Thanasset, and again when screwing up Gharlas's crazy plans seemed enough to do. Logical I had been, and wrong both times.

I couldn't help feeling there might be something more, something I didn't know yet. That suspicion generated frustration and a renewal of the cycle: why the hell had I been stuck in the middle of this?

Two days of that kind of thinking convinced me it was as bad as worrying about Tarani and Keeshah. So I made another resolution: one step at a time. And the next step was, if possible, to get the Ra'ira out of here and back to Raithskar, where it could be guarded by men of honor. Focus on that, I told myself, and quit bugging yourself about things you can't possibly control.

Having thus made the decision not to think about the

things worth thinking about, for the next three days I was bored past imagining. I asked my silent guards for a set of mondeana. After three hours, I seemed to have exhausted all possible combinations of the six dice-like pieces. I inquired about reading material, but Gandalaran books are handwritten and precious; my guards snickered at the request. I did continue the calisthenics; they were all that kept my spirits up.

On the morning of the sixth day, I was told I would be seeing the High Lord.

I was allowed to bathe and given a change of clothing. It was an inexpressible relief to be clean. The loose-fitting desert outfit I had been wearing—dark green trousers with a tan tunic—resembled well-used dusting rags.

I knew, from its performance in my daily activities, that my arm was mostly healed, but it was still a pleasant surprise to wash away the dirt and find only a tracing of a scar zigzagging the area where the dralda's teeth had scored.

It was hardly surprising that I was given a guard's uniform to wear, considering where I was being held. All Gandalarans wore a variety of styles in trousers and/or tunics made from woven fabric. The elegance of any outfit was determined by the softness of the fabric, the quantity and delicacy of decorative work, and coordinated color combinations. Uniforms— that is, look-alike dress identified with a particular group— tended to be monotone. The Fa'aldu wore long white tunics. The Peace and Security Officers in Raithskar were identified by gray leather baldrics. The Sharith wore tan desert tunic and trousers, with the addition of colored sashes for rank identification.

The High Guard uniform was no exception: trousers slightly more fitted than the flowing desert style, and a sleeveless tunic, both in a mossy green. It was dressed up a bit more with boots and baldric of a dark leather that didn't match badly with my belt, which I was allowed to keep.

As I walked between my two guards out of the barracks toward the huge structure that was the traditional family home of the Harthim Lords—who, according to Eddartan law, were usually the High Lords, as well—it wasn't lost on me that I looked a whole lot like any other High Guard member.

Except that my companions each carried sword and dagger,

and I didn't have a weapon. Any sword would have felt good in my hand, but I wanted Rika back.

Thinking about the steel sword reminded me of Obilin, which turned my thoughts to Indomel, which made me wonder about Zefra, which generated a pang of anxiety over Tarani, which brought me full circle to Obilin again. I hadn't seen the man since he'd ordered my imprisonment. Absence hadn't made me any fonder of him. And that made me think of Rika again.

Quit fretting, I ordered my subconscious, which ignored me. *Indomel has some of the answers you want, and we're nearly there.*

We went into the Harthim house by the front door. I found I was surprised to find it fairly ordinary, though scaled slightly larger and richly furnished. My time in this house on my last trip had been spent in Zefra's quarters, in a back wing which bordered Pylomel's beautiful garden. Ricardo was expecting the High Lord himself to live like Louis XVI, surrounded by courtiers and flagrant wealth.

Maybe this was just Pylomel's influence, I thought. *All that gorgeous stuff hidden away in the treasure vault—Gharlas called it. Pylomel certainly was a hoarder. And Indomel hasn't had time to change anything, even if he wanted to.*

We went through the huge center room—in a more modest home, it would be called the midhall—and entered a small parlor. I was facing a huge double-doored entryway. The guards saw me into the parlor, then left me alone.

Not for long. Obilin opened the double doors and bowed mockingly.

"Do join us, Lakad."

Lakad was the name I had used to get into the High Guard. It was also the only name by which Indomel knew me.

So you're keeping my secret, are you, Obilin? I thought as I edged past the High Guardsman. *For your own purpose, of course. But I won't spoil it for you. The less Indomel knows about me, the better.*

6

Indomel was seated in a room that tried to create the illusion of informality and failed dismally. For one thing, the standard stone ledges were missing. The chairs—seven of them—had frames of wood, not the more common Eddartan material of bamboo-like reeds. The fabric which served as seat and back was thickly embroidered. Thread ends, poking up here and there, betrayed age and wear.

For another thing, the chair arrangement was designed to make Indomel the focus of the room.

Seven chairs—this must be an "unoffical" Council chamber, where the Lords really make their decisions. I'd certainly be able to think more clearly here than in the shadow of that tall bronze panel.

For me, the focus of the room wasn't Indomel—it was Tarani, standing with Zefra behind the young High Lord's chair.

I let out a great sigh of relief. Tarani looked well, if a little tense. The only thing that mattered to me right then was seeing the flash of joy that crossed her face as I came into the room. She regained her composure quickly; I took that as advice, and controlled my impulse to run right over Indomel and scoop her up in my arms.

A couple of other factors counseled me to restrain myself. This "parlor" felt like a courtroom. It spelled danger I couldn't predict.

It doesn't look as though Tarani's on trial here, I thought. *The way she's standing there with Zefra, both of them dressed formally, she seems more part of the jury. That would indicate that Indomel—trusts her? Not in a million years. At least that she's protected in some way. I don't want to screw that up for her.*

So between shame and speculation, I merely walked into the room and stood calmly in front of Indomel.

42

The boy had changed little since the last time I had seen him.

He bore a family resemblance to Tarani and Zefra. The delicacy of bone structure was less noticeable, in Indomel's face, than the flatness of his cheeks and the sharpness of his widow's peak. The tusks which occupied the position of human canine teeth seemed extraordinarily large because the other teeth were slightly smaller than normal. His eyes dominated the face, looming dark and large from underneath the minimal supraorbital ridge that seemed to be a Harthim characteristic.

Physically, he was nearly identical to the Indomel I had met in Lord Hall. But there was a subtle difference in his bearing. Then he had been a spoiled child—not a harmless one, as his secret connection with Obilin attested—but a child.

As the High Lord, he had more mature and cautious a bearing, but no less nasty a nature.

"Do sit down," he said. "One should not learn the manner of his death while standing."

It was an obvious attempt to rattle me, but I wasn't buying. I'd been living with the prospect of immediate death for the last six days. And I had the feeling he was just goading me.

"You aren't going to kill a man who just had his first bath in weeks," I said, taking the chair that was offered. Obilin remained standing by the door, looking extra alert. Tarani was watching us with interest. Zefra was staring out the window. Indomel and I were the only ones sitting.

"Perhaps we have fastidious executioners—had you not considered that, Lakad?"

Indomel really believes my name is Lakad. Not only has Obilin kept his mouth shut, but neither Tarani nor Zefra has been forced to reveal anything about me. I looked again at Zefra, who hadn't moved since I'd come into the room. She stared off out the window I faced, a disturbing blankness to her face. *Can that be an act?* I wondered. *Whatever it is, captive or not, Tarani still has some power over the High Lord.*

For the first time in six days, I started to feel hopeful.

"You forget, High Lord," I said, managing not to pronounce the title sarcastically, "that I've had dealings with the High Guard. I'd say that, given the chance to kill somebody, they'd be much less interested in style than in efficiency."

Indomel laughed at that, and relaxed back into his chair.

"You have described yourself, my friend. For did you not enroll in the High Guard, just before the unfortunate death of my father? You are not yet released from that duty and you shall be placed, at Obilin's request, directly under his supervision."

I looked at Obilin, who couldn't quite hide a smirk of satisfaction.

"Obilin appropriated... the sword I was carrying," I said. "May I have it back?"

"A bold request," Indomel said, not missing the fact that Obilin and I weren't the best of friends. "Especially from a man who could as easily be executed as hired. Were it not that the lady Tarani has convinced me that the third member of your group, a man whom Zefra identified as Sharith, was actually and independently responsible for Pylomel's death—"

"Sharith?" Obilin interrupted, taking a step into the room. "Then there *were* sha'um?"

Obilin's surprise was welcome. *It's clear that Obilin and Indomel haven't talked to each other much. Now, if I can just keep it straight about who knows what...*

"A sha'um," I corrected him. "It left with Thymas."

"Your friend abandoned you so readily?" Indomel said, then smiled. "Ah, I think I see. The lady Tarani was a source of conflict between you. As I believe she is between you and Obilin. Am I right, Guardsman?" he asked, looking at the little man with amusement as Obilin's face darkened. "Of course I am right."

Indomel stood up and paced slowly inside the wide semicircle of chairs. He was wearing a floor-length tunic and vest, tied with a jeweled rope; there was a soft clinking as the rope ends swung against each other in response to his movement.

"I welcome the attachment between you and the lady Tarani," he said. "Because it offers me certain assurances. She has been most persuasive in her efforts to keep you alive, and has made certain—uh—concessions on your behalf."

"Concessions"? I wondered. I had a heart-sinking memory of Pylomel and his peculiar appetites. *Surely not his own sister,* I argued with myself. *Or would he have taken Obilin's part... God, no!*

"You will have heard that I am of a thrifty nature, Lakad. It seemed wasteful to provide food and shelter to a strong and healthy man, whose fighting skill has been well proven—

44

hence the decision to, um, extend your enlistment in the Guard."

He paused in front of my chair. "The lady Tarani is being treated with honor," he said, "but that could change at any time. Only those of us in this room—yes, I am aware of Obilin's knowledge—know that I have a natural *elder* sister. Should even a rumor of this reach beyond the five of us, Tarani's comfort will be threatened. Should you fail your assigned duties as a High Guardsman, she will suffer. If you try to escape, she will die. Is that stated clearly enough?"

"Yes," I said. I was trembling. I dared not look at Tarani.

Indomel nodded, seemed to relax, and then smiled broadly.

"As to your specific assignment," he said, "I was faced with a dilemma, caused by Obilin's personal feelings toward you and the lady Tarani."

Obilin stiffened at the sound of amusement in the High Lord's voice.

"On the one hand," Indomel continued, "Obilin is *totally* loyal to me, and will in all things obey my wishes." The High Lord moved over to the small man, at least fifteen years older than himself, and put his hand on Obilin's shoulder.

Ricardo had once seen a human pat a dog on the head with just that air of condescension. Obilin reacted in just about the same way—except that his ears wouldn't fold back.

"On the other hand," said Indomel, "I have a great deal of sympathy for his admiration of my sister and his hatred of you, and I would prefer to spare *him* the embarrassment of letting his feelings violate his loyalty. I have promised, after all, that you shall *live*.

"Therefore, you shall report to Obilin directly, as he requests, but from a distance. As of this moment, you will be in charge of the Lingis copper mine."

I don't know who was more startled, Obilin or me.

"Me? Supervising slaves? I won't do it!" I exclaimed.

Indomel laughed. "It sounds as though you've been talking to those stupid Raithskarians," he said, then whirled on Obilin, his mood change swift as lightning. "Go prepare the transfer orders. He will leave immediately."

I had to hand it to Obilin. The rug had just been pulled out from under him, but he recovered quickly, betraying his reaction only in a slight shakiness in his voice. "Naddam, the present supervisor, is a good man, High Lord. What reason shall I give for replacing him?"

45

"Think of something," Indomel shouted. "The death rate among his slaves is higher than anywhere else. Tell him it's punishment for working them too hard. Tell him it's reward for such devotion to his work. Just *write the order.*"

It was unquestionable a dismissal. The High Guardsman backed out of the room and closed the double doors, glaring at me all the way.

"Raithskar," Indomel said, and took a deep breath to calm the rage he had let us glimpse. "The name reminded me of a matter which does not concern Obilin." The High Lord went to a shelf area on the wall behind me and lifted a wooden box. He set it on a lower shelf, opened it with his back to us, and turned around with both fists closed.

"Where," he asked, "did you get this?" He opened his left hand to display a blue jewel, darker blue lines hinting at a crystalline structure deep within it. Tarani and I both gasped.

There seemed no point in hiding that part of the story. I had twisted in the chair to watch his movements. I turned back around and spoke with my back to the High Lord.

"Gharlas stole it from Raithskar," I said. "We got it from him."

"Not this one, you didn't," Indomel said. He came into the center of the grouped chairs, kicked aside the edge of the carpet and threw the jewel hard at the marble-slabbed floor. It shattered with a surprisingly soft sound.

"Glass, as I discovered shortly after you left Eddarta—at least, as I suspected, when my dear mother proved to be over-confident of her powers. I took it from her, reserving judgment on the gem in favor of further experimentation. She . . ."

He looked at Zefra, who merely stared back at him, unflinching. She hadn't yet said a word.

"The lady Zefra was punished for her temerity, I assure you. My next thought," Indomel continued, "was to wonder how the three of you had arrived in the Council Chamber. It was unthinkable that no one would have seen you enter, equally unthinkable that anyone, seeing a stranger go into the Council Chamber, would not alert the guard.

"There *are* two doors into that room. It is well known among the Harthim that Troman's Way exists, though its secret has long been lost to us. Once I suspected you had somehow discovered it, and entered the Council Chamber *through* the treasure vault, I was understandably anxious to verify that the treasure was intact. By that time, I could hear the other Lords shouting about Pylomel's death and searching for me, but I thought it wise to inspect the vault first."

He took a deep breath. "As it turned out, it was *very* wise. Only *I* know that Gharlas was killed *inside* the vault, instead of at the foot of the Bronze, where the others found his body. (A poetic statement, of sorts, isn't it? Yet I was less concerned with symbolism at the time than with the weight of my dead uncle's bones.)

"Only *I* know," he said, his voice rising slightly, "that the High Lord's treasure has been systematically pilfered, all the jewelry and gemstones replaced by *glass imitations*. It was at that moment that I began to suspect the truth—that an imitation Ra'ira had been left here, to inspire my mother to over-tax her abilities in trying to control me. A wonderful thing, the mind. Because she and I both believed she had the true Ra'ira, she did actually succeed—temporarily.

"One doesn't imitate what is not real, and the real Ra'ira must have been present in that room, to allow . . . my *sister* to read the Bronze. That meant that you *still* had it."

He smiled—a little bitterly, I thought—and opened his other hand. "Now *I* have it."

7

"And," the High Lord added, "I am most anxious to hear how and why it escaped from Raithskar, how it was duplicated, and how it arrived here."

He was only asking for my life story for the past two months or so. I hesitated answering merely because I didn't know where to start. Tarani said nothing.

"In the space of three breaths, you three will be the next meal for the dralda," he said fiercely. *"Answer!"*

"Gharlas wanted to—" I broke off before I finished the thought.

No point in giving him the idea of "world conquest" if he doesn't already have it, I reminded myself.

"—control Eddarta through controlling you," I finished, hoping the pause hadn't been too noticeable. "He spent a long time planning to get the Ra'ira. He had—" Another pause, to avoid saying Volitar's name. "—the same person who duplicated the gemstones make a duplicate. Two duplicates were actually made. Gharlas took one to Raithskar, but managed to lose it before he could switch it for the real one—so he just stole the real one.

"Later, he realized it probably wouldn't do for anyone else to claim having the Ra'ira. The first one was lost and harmless, but he went back to get the other duplicate. He killed the man who had made it, but didn't actually get it. We had the duplicate; we followed Gharlas here, and—well, you already know we gave you the imitation Ra'ira in order to get ourselves out of here."

Indomel considered what I had said, working his fingers gently around the Ra'ira.

So close, I moaned to myself. *I wonder, if I jumped him* . . . Tarani caught my eye and shook her head, very slightly. *She may not be able to read minds,* I thought, *but she's getting damned good at reading me. What does she*

48

think we can do from more than a hundred miles apart? The copper *mines, for heaven's sake!*

I felt the edges of despair closing in on me. It was becoming a familiar feeling. Indomel snapped my attention back to him.

"As far as it goes," he said, "your tale is believable, and I accept it. But none of it tells me what I most want to know." He walked over to where I was sitting and looked straight down into my eyes.

I forced myself to look back, into the dark iris and the peculiar, familiar glow behind the pupil, and suddenly I had to fight hard to keep still and control the panic that bubbled at the edges of my mind.

He's going to try his mindpower on me—a compulsion—I can feel it—God! He's as strong as Gharlas, if not stronger— but I've had practice now; he can't control me—but I don't want him to know that!—Keeshah, I wish you were still with me, just for the comfort—Oh, Lord and Grandmama Marie, let me do this right . . .

"How did Gharlas know that the Ra'ira has special powers?" Indomel asked, a slight tremor disrupting the solemn note of command in his voice.

I let my eyes go slightly out of focus, opened my mouth a couple of times as though I were struggling against the compulsion (as, indeed, I was—only more successfully than I pretended), then said, slowly: "He said he found a book in the vault—a journal of the ancient kings—that described what the Ra'ira could do and how it was used."

"I have examined every article in the vault," Indomel said. "There is no such book."

That wasn't a question, so I didn't say anything.

"Where is that book now?" Indomel asked.

"I don't know," I answered, telling the absolute truth.

"Did it—no, you wouldn't know that, either," Indomel said, more to himself than to me. He broke the eye contact for a moment and stared thoughtfully at the jewel and his fingers as they moved, turning the Ra'ira in his hand. "Gharlas would have planned carefully, studied its keeping in Raithskar— there is nothing special in the theft itself, I suppose. It is only remarkable that it took a fool like Gharlas to think of bringing it back to Eddarta."

There was something special in the theft, I thought to myself. *But you don't need to know that Gharlas seemed to have the rarest of mindgifts—the ability to actually read the thoughts of another Gandalaran. I ought to tell you, just for spite, but it wouldn't be in character.*

Indomel turned to me again, and I stiffened under his spooky stare. "Gharlas would have no reason to lie to you," he said, "so the book he spoke of must exist, and he must have removed it from the vault.

"That could have been done only through Troman's Way. The guards who searched Gharlas's home had no more fortune in finding the entrance than has anyone else in the generations since Troman used that passageway to meet his women. If you came *through* it, you know how to get *into* it—tell me."

"The door is on the right-hand side of the entry door," I said. "A wall panel slides back, and you go through sideways to a small landing, and then stairs. But Gharlas opened it, and I couldn't do it again."

"How did he open it?" Indomel demanded.

"Pressure on the nearby floor tiles, a complicated pattern. I couldn't tell you which tiles, what order—anything about it, only that I'm pretty sure that's the way he opened the door."

Indomel thought about that. "The vault has similar tiles, that date from about the same period," he mused. "The same method—where is the vault door located?" he asked.

"Behind the big tapestry—on the other side of the vault from where you must have found Gharlas's body. That's as close as I can pinpoint it."

Indomel smiled. "Well, I expect that's sufficient. It is only a matter of time before I can discover the correct combination."

It's only a matter of time, I thought, *before a computerized random selection of alpha characters and spaces recreates Hamlet's soliloquy. A matter of a lot of time. Good luck.*

"One more question," Indomel said. "Why are you involved in this?"

Uh-oh. I blinked dazedly at Indomel for about three seconds, worrying furiously the entire time. Then I thought: *Sorry, Tarani, but this seems the safer course.*

"The man who made the duplicate Ra'ira was Volitar." At the edge of my vision, I saw Zefra twitch. Tarani never moved a muscle. "I met Tarani and Thymas on their way to visit him,

50

when they still thought Volitar was her father. I tagged along because of Tarani, and happened to be there...Gharlas killed Volitar, but couldn't force Tarani to give him the second duplicate. Between her looks and her power, Gharlas figured out that Tarani was Zefra's daughter. Tarani was determined to come to Eddarta to meet Zefra and defeat Gharlas's plans. Thymas and I came with her...to protect her," I ended, unable to hide the bitterness I felt.

Some of that was true, some false. But it seemed to satisfy Indomel, and I marked that down as one assessment of his character: *He likes simple solutions*.

"All right," he said, and I felt the compulsion drop away abruptly.

I relaxed with a sigh of relief. Accepting that compulsion without really responding to it had been a terrific strain. I wasn't sure what "mental muscles" I used at times like that, but I knew it cost a lot of energy. But I wasn't griping. I felt, in fact, as though I was really ahead, for a change—I'd kept Indomel ignorant of my specialness.

The feeling of victory vanished when Indomel put away the Ra'ira, stepped into the waiting area, and opened the outer door. "Get Obilin," he ordered, then came back into the room. "You may now say your farewells to the lady Tarani," he said. "It *is* the last time you will see her."

Protests of all kinds gathered in my throat, but I put them aside for the one thing which seemed immediately important. "Can we speak privately?" I asked.

"I'm sure that Obilin is eager to accept charge of you, *Guardsman*," he said. "Don't waste what time you have making ridiculous requests."

Tarani had moved around the chairs; I stood up to meet her. She was guarded, restrained, conscious of the people watching. I was full of grief and guilt and bitterness. In silence, I pulled her into my arms.

There was no passion between us in that moment, but an acknowledgment of linkage, of bonding, of being a single unit no matter what physical distance separated us. And somehow, in the midst of every evil thing that surrounded us and the seemingly impossible struggle that faced us, there was comfort. We didn't kiss, but merely held each other, her body pliant and soft, her embrace as strong as mine.

The door opened. Tarani stirred and pressed her cheek against mine. So softly that I barely caught the words, Tarani

51

whispered: *"There is hope."* Then she moved away from me, leaving a giant coldness where she had been.

The way to Lingis was straight, hard, and boring. I had a lot of time, in those five days, to remember the final few seconds of the interview with Indomel, the picture of the room indelible in my mind: Obilin stony-faced, Zefra still immobile, Indomel sort of blank-looking. All of them loomed in my remembered vision like statues; even I seemed frozen. Only Tarani was alive, breathing, warm. She glowed with vitality, and promise, and a curious sort of peace.

There is hope, she had said.

Obilin had led me directly from the house to the gate of Lord City, where a group of guards waited with full backpacks and a lot of suppressed questions. We had stopped just out of their hearing range.

"They will take you to Lingis," Obilin had said. "Naddam will be expecting you in five days, and it is worth the girl's life for not to be even an hour late. He will show you the routine before he leaves. Be sure the mine continues to produce as well, but never forget that *you are as much a prisoner there as the slaves are.*"

He had given me a sword, and a folded, wax-sealed sheet of paper. I had put the sword through my baldric, aware of Obilin's alertness, fighting the tempting vision of the sword lashing out, of Obilin falling into his own blood. I had been sickened by the savagery of the image, even more so by the pleasure I felt in anticipation of its execution. That, and the background awareness of the consequences to Tarani, had guided the sword safely and unblooded to its place.

"There is a clerk," Obilin had continued, after a slight hesitation. I had wondered if he had been disappointed that I hadn't tried something. "He sends daily reports directly to the High Lord; he has been instructed to see you every day; the first day he misses you will be the last day of Tarani's life."

He had spoken savagely, and I had seen a new truth—part of Obilin's hatred, now at least, was concern for Tarani's welfare. I had control of her fate, and Obilin was losing control of mine. At least, so it had seemed to Obilin and to me.

"One last word," Obilin had said, gripping my arm painfully. "Remember that Naddam is not the only guard in Lingis who reports to me."

He had shoved me toward the group. The six guards—most of whom had been assigned to the rotating schedule around my confinement—had sandwiched me between two columns, and we had left Eddarta.

Naddam greeted me, in Lingis, with understandable resentment. Obilin's explanation—I got a glimpse of the message which had arrived by messenger bird the day I had left Eddarta with the "official" transfer orders—was patently transparent, and he wanted to know what was going on.

I didn't tell him anything, at first—but Naddam turned out to be a real surprise. He had the same tough-muscled, scarred look as most of the mine guards—generally not the pick of the crop—but Naddam was an intelligent man, as compassionate as his role would allow him to be.

The mine operated from a city-like enclosure two man-days away from the Lingis River for which it was named. Water was hauled in by vlek and stored in rooftop tanks to provide drinking water and an occasional bath.

The slaves were organized into semi-military groups, each of eight groups assigned to a small barracks. Each group had twelve to fifteen slaves and four guards, divided into two teams which alternated resting and working six-hour shifts broken up among the duties of actual mining, hauling, and loading ore, and "camp" duties like cooking, washing, and cleaning. During any given seven-day, one of the slave groups would have it slightly easier on "vlek" duty. Team A wrestled half the work animals into delivering ore to the foundry in Tarling and bringing back water, while Team B tended the other half and took care of the shorter hauling job of bringing mined ore into camp.

Naddam was explaining all this to me as he guided me through the barracks area.

"Every group has more than just the twelve people necessary for both teams," I pointed out.

"To allow for illness," he snapped.

"Or death?" I asked, and Naddam pulled up short. "I heard," I continued, "that the death rate among slaves is higher here than in the other mines."

The Guardsman looked at me squarely, his hands on his hips. He wasn't a young man, as the darkening areas of his yellowish headfur betrayed. "My people get hot meals, regular rest, and more comfort than in the other mines," he said.

"As you'd know, if you had any mine experience at all." He turned away in disgust.

The explanation he didn't offer then arrived the next day in the form of a group of slaves being transferred from a mine further north: three men and a woman, all skin and bones, standing unsteadily, coughing violently. Naddam greeted their guards at the gate of the compound with something less than politeness, gruffly directed them to the dining hall, and called his own guards to take the newcomers to their assigned barracks. He caught the woman and supported her during a coughing fit, then handed her to a guard with a gentle touch.

8

Naddam walked back to where he had left me, near the command barracks; the gentleness I had seen in his handling of the woman vanished in an explosion of anger.

"Of course the death rate here is higher," he growled. "Every other mine works their people to death, and then—then, as a gesture of kindness—they send the dying ones here to 'recover'. They *might* recover, with total rest and constant care, but I can't afford that—not in wasting them as manpower and not in the resentment of the other slaves. So I put them on the lightest duty I can, give them extra food portions and as much rest as possible—and, of course, they die anyway. And a 'death' that belongs somewhere else shows up on my record!"

"You're not worried about your record," I said.

"*What?*" Nammad demanded. He must have seen something of what I was thinking in my face, because he repeated the word less belligerently. "What?"

"You're concerned for *them*," I said, waving my arm in the direction the slaves had gone. "I'd have seen it before, if I hadn't been looking at everything from the slaves' point of view, hating the work and the place and the confinement. I'll bet your record for slaves who *survive* their sentence and go free is higher than anywhere else, too."

"That's right," Naddam said. "And you're here to change all that, right?" But there was less conviction than question in the remark.

"Wrong. I'm here because Indomel sent me. I can't tell you why, because doing that will endanger somebody I care about."

Naddam nodded. "I thought Obilin's letter sounded a little out of joint. I'm not being thrown out, is that it? You're being thrown *in?*"

"That's about the size of it. I think you've figured out that I don't like the idea any more than you do. But it seems as

55

though you're giving the slaves the best break they can expect. I want to keep that up, Naddam. Show me how to do things your way."

He was quiet for a moment, studying me. "I been doing this for ten years," he said at last. "It's not bad duty—the women are grateful for decent treatment." He put his hand on my shoulder, the first time he had touched me. "But now that I know these folks won't see much change for the worse, I'm kinda looking forward to city duty. I'll tell you all I can," he promised.

In the remaining few days of his tenure, Naddam showed me every phase of the mining operation, explaining with some pride that Lingis was unique among the copper mines.

There were seven mines located from Lingis northward along a line that followed the base of the steep mountain range that marked this portion of the "wall" around Gandalara. Only the Lingis ore lode was close to the surface and reasonably shallow. The others used the same techniques I saw at Lingis, but to less advantage as they followed narrow lodes into the sides of mountains.

In Lingis, the people worked in air and daylight, and most of what they did was directly related to mining ore. The mine itself was a series of trenches, six to twenty feet deep, that ridged a hillside, with the newest trench also the highest. The effort of the work crews was divided about equally into three parts. A third worked the current trench, breaking the mountainside into large chunks with stone hammers and bronze pick-like tools. Another third hauled the chunks downhill and broke them down into manageable pieces. That was done by brute force; four people lifted a huge column of rock and dropped it, lifted and dropped, until a big rock was pulverized into pieces no bigger than my fist.

The rest of the crews worked at opening the next trench, and that process was intricate and time-consuming. Once the rock had been laid bare of topsoil and salt layer (much thinner here than it seemed to be in the Gandalaran deserts, where the Fa'aldu built their homes of three-foot salt-block cubes), an engineer studied the face of the hillside and marked a line with mild acid. Drilling crews placed a six-foot rod of bronze, mounted in a wood frame to stay vertical, over a point on the line. The rod was about six inches in diameter, and its tip was crusted with rock powder. It started digging into the acid scar when the crew pushed the shoulder-high turning spokes, and didn't stop until a hole fifteen inches deep had been drilled—except for breaks to flush out the rock debris with water. Then it moved on to a new spot.

When there were holes at two-foot intervals all along the line the engineer had drawn, the holes were stuffed tightly with three-foot reeds that had been split, wet, and tightly rolled. The reeds were allowed to dry until they were stiff and hard.

I happened to be there on a "new trench" day. All other work stopped, both for the safety of the rest of the crew and because it was an impressive sight to watch.

The trench-opening crew stood above the reed-stuffed holes and worked in close coordination with one another. At each hole, two or three people placed a thin bronze rod with a pointed tip into the center of the stiff reeds, waggled it carefully until it was well seated, then forced it deeper into the opening by measured taps with a rock hammer. The ringing sound of stone on bronze was the only noise on the hillside. The workers didn't strike simultaneously, or even in any detectable rhythm, but there was an inescapable feeling of teamwork to the sound. The blows seemed to slow, become heavier—and then another sound drowned them out. One crack, two, then a series of popping and cracking sounds that grew into a deafening noise.

The work crew jumped backward as, all along the line the engineer had etched, the hillside split open.

I felt like cheering, but I seemed to be the only one, and I realized that, for the rest of them, that feat of engineering just meant more work.

Still, it took only one talk with the engineer to convince me that Lingis duty was, truly, the easiest of all the mines. Elsewhere the "trenches" were only part of the job—as they led into the mountain, the over-hanging rock, too, had to be dismantled. At Tarnel, the oldest of the mines, the working trench was a combination chasm and unsupported tunnel, and the crews worked in dust-choked, dangerous conditions that provoked the coughing disease that claimed so many of the slaves.

So Lingis was blessed with easy access to its ore, as well as a humane manager. Under those circumstances, it didn't surprise me that it was the most productive. And *that* made it no surprise that the Lingis profits went to the High Lord's family.

Naddam spent several days showing me around and introducing me to guards—a group Ricardo would have named a "motley crew". On his last night at the mine, he invited me to his rooms for a few glasses of *barut*, the Gandalaran equivalent of whiskey, made from a fermented grain and not bad as booze went. I left his rooms—soon to be mine—late, with the remainder of the bottle as a farewell gift, grateful for Naddam's sympathy and hopeful that the barut would help me get to sleep.

My Gandalaran "inner awareness" had been telling me I wasn't sleeping enough, but it could only warn. It couldn't force compliance on a mind bent on self-pity and worry.

During the days, the company of Naddam and the mental activity of learning what he had to tell me had kept me pretty well occupied. But even then, examining production charts or viewing the mining operation, I frequently found my breath snatched away and my chest squeezed by a flash vision of Tarani, alone in Eddarta. At night, there were no distractions.

Tonight I was so tired that I found it difficult to worry about one thing at a time, and I was swept through a dizzying assortment of images, each one plunging me deeper into depression. Tarani as I had last seen her—in control but threatened by Indomel and Obilin, Zefra an unknown quantity offering little hope. *Keeshah turning away from me*. Naddam, a friendly figure, but threatening in that his protection would be absent tomorrow.

One of the most tormenting visions—the memory of Obilin in the desert, tracing the outline of Tarani's breast with the point of his sword—had me in its grip when I heard a noise outside the closed shutters of my bedroom window. The shutters didn't rattle. There was no real *sound* to the noise at all, merely a whooshing, like wind.

But the only wind I'd encountered in Gandalara was in the high passes that formed the Chizan crossing.

I heard it again and, grateful for the distraction, I went to the window and opened the shutters. I had to clamp down a shout of surprise and pleasure—Lonna was hovering, patiently waiting to be admitted. The sound I had heard was the sweeping of her big wings.

The white bird sailed past me into the room, and I closed the shutters. She swung around the room once, her wingspread making her seem to fill the room, then she slammed into my chest, knocking me over. She made one sound—the soft, hooting sound I had learned to associate with pleasure—then remained silent. But it wasn't the bird's nature to be inexpressive; for a few seconds I was blinded by flapping white feathers, the skin of my ribs and legs both tickled and pricked by her claws as Lonna jumped all over me.

For my part, I was nearly as happy to see her. She would have been welcome in herself as a "friendly face", so to speak. But the manner of her approach—so silent, so wary—could mean only one thing. Tarani had sent her to me. The bird's arrival meant that I wasn't as alone as I felt, and neither was Tarani.

I took all the time necessary to calm and cuddle Lonna, since that was the only reward I could offer her. Then, so eagerly that I was shaking, I took the bulky band from her leg and opened the letter from Tarani.

Rikardon,

I cannot risk sending Lonna to you often, but this one time I must. The situation in Eddarta is not what it seems. Indomel believes that his cruel punishment of my mother has damaged her permanently, and he no longer fears her. But in this he is deceived. Even before I returned, Zefra's daze was partly pretended; with my power to aid her, she is herself again. Indomel underestimates us both.

Free yourself, and take no thought for my safety, my love. No matter what Indomel said, I am in no danger from him. Zefra and I together can protect ourselves from his mindpower, should it come to that. But my brother keeps me well for his own reasons—he has failed in every attempt to use the Ra'ira. He believes I used its power when I read the Bronze, and though I have convinced him that I must have done so unconsciously and cannot school him in skills I do not have, he wishes to win my willing assistance in mastering the gem. I have let him think I am trying, and so have traded something worthless for the thing most precious to me—your life.

In doing this, I gained some time for us all, though it dwindles daily as Indomel grows more impatient. I say again that Indomel cannot harm me; I fear only that his spite will separate me from my mother, or that his vengeance will strike at you. Zefra and I have talked and

59

*planned; there is a way to defeat Indomel, but we must
act soon. Free yourself, and come to me. Through Lonna's
eyes I will know when to expect you, and I will send her
to guide you to me.*

It will seem years before we meet, my love.

—Tarani.

I thought a lot of things about that letter as I read it and
re-read it by lamplight.

Our names are on it, I thought. *What if Lonna had been
caught?* Then, sentimental as a schoolboy, I was shocked and
thrilled by two words: *"My love"*. She called me *"my love"*.

But mostly, the words in the letter confirmed what would
have been my own hunch, if I'd been able to lasso all the
wandering thoughts together in some logical order. Indomel
hadn't acted like someone who had just laid his hands on a
worldkiller.

He must have tried to read the Bronze himself, I decided.
*Probably really burns him that Tarani could do it and he
can't. Tarani said that any help from the Ra'ira came
subconsciously, and I believe her. Considering the fact that
Indomel's gift is pretty strong, and he's having trouble, it
must take a little time to get the hang of using that thing
when and how you want to.*

*I'd like to think it has the fairy-tale quality of only working
for the good guys, but what I know of Gandalaran history
proves that idea's a crock. The reason the Ra'ira was in
Raithskar in the first place was because it had been misused
by the last of the Kings.*

Indomel's direct ancestor. It figures.

Now don't say that, I chided myself. *Harthim was Tarani's
ancestor, too—in blood, if not in spirit. It's ironic, really,
that the only person who might lead the way the good Kings
did doesn't want any part of the Ra'ira.*

*So there's a balance of power in Eddarta, in many levels of
meaning. And Tarani says she's safe. Can I believe her?*

That question helped me put my finger on one of the
things that had been bothering me most. In the desert, I had
stubbornly dragged Tarani into captivity. Afterward, another
pendulum swing of my irrational mind had let me dump all
the responsibility on her. I hadn't questioned her leadership
continuing in Eddarta because Tarani could deal from a
stronger hand than mine. But squirming away in the back of

my mind was a nasty little thought, a suspicion that I had won Tarani's undying contempt.

What am I thinking? I wondered. *Be logical, at least. If she were really trying to sacrifice herself for me, she'd have said: "Break out of that there hoose-gow and high-tail it for home!" But she said to get away and come to Eddarta Therefore she's safe, logically.*

But logic be hanged, damn it! I thought. *What about trust? She said she's safe; therefore she is safe. I've got to get rid of this guilt complex; it's making me see Tarani's motives through a mirror.*

What did she say in the letter? I wondered, searching for the remembered line.

"Free yourself soon," she says.

Not "if you can."

"When to expect you."

Not "if you survive."

Bless her, I thought, my throat so choked that I'd have been crying, if Gandalarans could weep for emotional reasons. *She still believes in me.*

Then I've got to believe in myself.

The problem is, how do I get out of here? I'm not guarded, but if I leave, you can bet I'll be followed. That wimp Tullen—the clerk Obilin mentioned, an unlikable person— will notify Indomel first thing, of course. There's nothing I can do about that, and Tarani seems to think she can handle Indomel. All I have to do is get my body away from here in one piece.

I walked to the wall pegs where my belt was hanging. I touched it, let it fall across my palm. I was sure the circular shapes would escape the notice of anyone who didn't know the belt was filled with memorial Eddartan gold coins.

There's more than one kind of power, I thought.

For the first time since I'd come to Lingis, I spent a sleepless night profitably.

I sent Lonna back with a brief note. It didn't say much more than

Thanks for writing; I'll get there as soon as I can.

Everything else I wanted to say kept phrasing itself gushily, and I decided I'd save Lonna the weight, me the frustration, and that message for personal delivery.

61

9

The next morning, the camp-duty guards and I turned out to wish Naddam a good trip and pleasant duty. When he had gone, I looked over the group I now "commanded".

"I know it's no secret to you," I said, "that my coming here wasn't my choice. But that fact is, I was put *in charge*, and I am *in charge*."

I watched them carefully. Several sets of eyes looked away from me and seemed to watch what one man would do—a tall guy named Jaris.

"For the time being, things will continue exactly as Naddam set them up," I said. "I'm not about to mess with success, at least not until I'm sure any changes will be improvements. Jaris, bring the work schedule and duty roster to my office. The rest of you—back to your assignments."

I walked away, my spine tingling from the weight of their stares.

Jaris came into the room in Naddam's quarters that was designated as his office—a broad table and a few chairs, shelves on one wall for rosters, and production records. Jaris was a youngish man for mine work, barely into his twenties, I thought. He was tall and kind of thin, but his slim frame carried whipcords of muscle. I hadn't been able to figure out whether it was a gesture of unity or one of defiance, but the Lingis guards consistently wore only the trousers of the High Guard uniform. Two baldrics—one for sword, one for dagger, lay across Jaris's smooth chest. He adjusted his dagger to rest on the top of his thigh when he sat down at my invitation.

I took the rosters he offered me, but set them aside unread. I let him fidget for a few seconds while I stared at him.

No reason, I thought, *that he shouldn't be as nervous as I am. This has to be right; it doesn't figure any other way.*

"Ever heard of the Living Death, Jaris?" I asked.

"Who?" he said, almost casually. But I had seen the fractional start he had quickly controlled.

I guessed right, I thought with relief. *Now if I can just handle this right . . .*

"I thought so," I said, and stood up to walk over to the window. The slaves who had today's "domestic" assignment were moving about, collecting night waste from the barracks, tending the vleks. One of the men who had arrived recently staggered out of the barracks to which he'd been sent, tried to call to one of the guards, and fell to coughing. His voice had been nearly inaudible at that distance, but the harsh rasping of his cough crackled across the space.

"All the dying ones come here first," I said, "which means the Living Death—recruited from among the dying slaves—have to escape from here. Lingis has a high death toll; I've seen the records. How many of those corpses are still alive, Jaris? I know Naddam well enough that he wouldn't have the stomach to handle the bodies himself—so you do it, and you don't check real close, do you?"

Jaris dropped the pretense of ignorance. He also dropped his other hand to the hilt of his sword.

"What about it?" he asked.

I shrugged. "Not much, really. I just like to understand things, that's all. And there's something that puzzles me. Molik paid Obilin, and Obilin paid you, right? And now it's Worfit who's footing the bill?"

"Yeah," he said, then repeated: "What about it?"

I hooked my fingers in my belt, crossed my legs, leaned against the windowsill. "I said I've seen the figures," I answered. "And *between* Molik and Worfit, there was no change in the death rate. Now, I have a proposition for you, but I'd hesitate to do business with a man who might have killed ten or twenty innocent people, just so that a change in statistics wouldn't make the wrong people suspicious."

"What's your proposition?" he asked warily.

"First answer the question," I said. "Were those other deaths your doing?"

He shifted in his chair. "You a friend of Obilin's?" he asked.

There was no deception in the way I laughed at that suggestion, and Jaris sensed it.

"Arright," he said. "Arright. I don't work exclusive for Obilin. You're right—there was three seven-days or so when

63

Obilin shut down his operation. I just doubled up on my other business, that's all. I didn't kill nobody."

"Other business?" I repeated, then rocked to my feet, unable to believe the conclusion I'd reached. "*You're* an agent for the Fa'aldu?"

Jaris was out of his chair, his dagger in his hand. "For a stranger, you sure know a lot. Just who the fleabite are you?"

I held up both hands, palms toward Jaris. "Easy now, I was just surprised, that's all. As to who I am—you don't want to know, Jaris. It can only get you into trouble."

"Yeah," he said, and relaxed a bit—but he didn't put away his blade. "Yeah, I got a feeling you're right. So tell me what you want, and let's get this done with."

"I want *out* of here," I said, putting real desire in the words. "But I need to know what I'd be getting *into*."

He considered me for a moment. "You already know about Obilin. The phony stiffs go straight to Eddarta and he takes them from there. The Fa'aldu business—goes by another route."

"Surely the Fa'aldu don't *pay* you," I said, thinking of the way they lived, trading, never using coins.

"Not them, the slave's relatives, friends, whatever. The Fa'aldu do the planning, and take the fee—I get it when the slave reaches the end of the line, some place in Chizan."

"Why Chizan?"

He laughed, a short, snorting sound. "You know what happens to somebody who's caught *after* escaping? This side of the world's filled with lowlifes looking to make a fast zak." He grinned, knowing I might put him in that same catagory. "The slaves who been in the mines—they all have a certain look, y'know? Somebody spots 'em, turns 'em in for a standing reward for returned slaves. Guards go anywhere to get 'em back—anywhere this side of Chizan."

I picked up the two gold coins I'd removed from my belt and left on the windowsill, and I held them so that the light gleamed from them. "Will this buy my passage out of here?" I asked Jaris. "Naturally, I'd prefer the Fa'aldu route."

"Naturally," Jaris said, as he stepped forward, holding out his hand. I pulled the coins back. "You wanna do business or not?" he snarled.

"I said before that I want to know what I'm getting into. Where do the Fa'aldu slaves go?"

"I take 'em to Taling when it's my turn to haul," he said,

grudgingly. "The Fa'aldu have a contact there—from that point to Chizan, I got no idea where they go."

"How do you account for them being gone?"

"Well, y'know, it's a funny thing about that long trip to Taling. Folks that look just as healthy as a vlek sometimes fall right over dead all of a sudden. And there ain't no point in bringing a corpse all the way back here, now is there?"

"When do you have hauling duty again?" I asked.

He grinned. "Now ain't you just in luck. I got to head out for Taling tomorrow."

He reached for the coins again; this time I let one of them drop into his palm.

"Hey!" he said.

"I want the name of the Fa'aldu contact in Taling," I said.

"When we get there," he growled. "You must think I'm stupid; I ain't gonna tell you that till we get to Taling."

"And the deal's off until I know that name," I said.

He tossed the gold coin and caught it. "I got half your money, man," he said.

"And I am not as squeamish as Naddam," I answered. "I don't much like this place, but while I'm here, I plan to do a thorough job. In fact, I will be checking dead bodies personally to be sure they're dead, and reporting any discrepancies *immediately* to Eddarta. Also, until further notice, you're suspended from water-hauling duty."

His eyes narrowed and I tensed, afraid for a moment that he'd let his anger get the better of him.

"A baker named Rull," Jaris said. "His shop is on the north side of town, the southeast corner of a small square."

I tossed him the other coin. "Tomorrow, then," I said. "I'll change clothes with one of the slaves, so—if you should ever be asked—you didn't even know I went along."

Jaris tucked the coins into his belt.

"I ain't gonna miss you much, Lakad," he said as he went to the door.

"It's mutual," I replied.

When he had left, my knees went weak with relief, and I sagged into the chair behind the desk.

It was worth the money for the misdirection, I thought. *Now when they find me gone in the morning, I'm hoping Jaris will think I've headed for Lingis, that the money was a bribe for the Fa'aldu contact's name, and that the main trickery was in the timing. I'm betting he'll lead everybody in that direction, bent on revenge.*

Most of all, I'm counting on the fact that Jaris is no smarter than he looks.

That unsettling thought was still with me that night, as I filled a makeshift pack with the portions of breakfast and lunch—both served to me in the office—which I had reserved. Fruit, bread, and cheese, and a few scraps of meat. I had been regularly, with no conscious intention, saving up the small, hard sweets that were served as dessert at the evening meals. Those, too, I packed, reflecting that they would come in handy as quick energy during my long run.

I hoped that it wouldn't occur to anyone that I would set off across the desert alone. These people were uniquely adapted for desert life, with a physical capability to retain water more efficiently than human beings. But water was still essential to their individual existence, even more so to community life. So their cities clustered around the rivers which spilled down from the Wall to irrigate land and quench thirst, and travel was, preferably, a matter of moving from city to city, following the contours of the Wall.

When desert travel was necessary, Gandalarans traveled in groups, lone travelers often waiting days for a caravan going in their direction, and paying in money or service for the chance to travel with the traders. Few Gandalarans felt it necessary to do what I was preparing to do now—endure days of heat and hunger and thirst, merely for the sake of getting from one place to another.

But few Gandalarans have the reasons I do, either, I mused as I tested the cork stopper in the ink bottle. I added the bottle and several sheets of parchment to the bundle I was piling on the cut-up blanket. *And fewer still have the experience of faster travel. Riding a sha'um makes you impatient with walking. If Keeshah were here, I'd be in Eddarta tomorrow night, instead of four days from now.* The thought made me feel slightly ashamed. The big cat was more, much more, than an animal of burden. *If Keeshah were here, this would all be easier,* I thought, the pain of loss ripping through me once again, as if he had only now left me. With it came another thought, full of anguish and fear.

Can that be the reason why I've fouled things up so badly? I wondered. *All the strength, the ability to think and plan, the leadership I had before—was that mine, or was it only on loan from Keeshah, through our linked minds? And did it go away with him?*

No! I fought the insecurity, shaking myself mentally. *I was Ricardo before I was Markasset, and I lived a full and decent life without Keeshah's help. His going hurt me, that's all. I've got to get used to the idea of life without him again—for his sake, as well as mine (and Tarani's). Because I know he couldn't control the time and place of his need to go.*

I had some excuse in the desert, I admitted to myself, *because of the suddenness of his loss. I was in shock. But if I let it get to me now, and interfere with Tarani's plans, then I'll be giving Keeshah responsibility for the consequences. It would hurt him—God, how it would hurt him—to think that his desertion had brought about my death.*

I wasn't fooling myself on one point—the next time Indomel got his hands on me, I'd die. I had to keep my wits about me, stay free, and—the truth of this shone out—die by my own hand rather than be used again as a weapon against Tarani.

As I fastened up the corners of the blanket, and used the long ends I had left free to tie the pack across my shoulders, anticipation and determination swept through me, making me feel more alert and awake than I had in days. I had felt the sensation before, at the moment when planning ended and action began. It was a carryover from Markasset, and it was well entrenched in Rikardon.

I slipped out the window, made my way through the torch-wavering shadows to the water tank, opened the tap, and drank deeply. Then I filled a small leather pouch, the only container I could bring without generating suspicion of my actual route. The cut-away part of the blanket was inside the pack, for the same reason—to leave no clues. The pouch wasn't prepared for water storage and would swell in the heat, stealing some of the precious liquid from me. Even with the special qualities of this Gandalaran body, I knew the water wouldn't be enough to last the entire journey, and I could look forward to a dismal last day.

I'll make it, I told myself, as I moved toward the stone wall of the enclosure. The wall wasn't extremely high—the surrounding desert was a much more effective barrier. *I know I'll make it. More importantly, Tarani knows it. She's counting on me, and I won't fail her again.*

I ducked back against one of the slave barracks as a

perimeter guard rounded the inner corner of the wall. He glanced in my direction, but the shadows hid me well enough. He was wearing such a look of boredom that I nearly pitied him.

When the guard had passed, I moved along the wall to the corner. The small spaces where the stone blocks met imperfectly were nearly useless elsewhere as hand- and toe-holds; there wasn't enough depth to them to support the vertical lifting of a man's body. But here, where one could brace between two walls, using the angle both for support while climbing and for greater pressure at each contact point, those spaces were sufficient.

Wheezing from the tension and exertion, the healed dralda wound throbbing in my arm from the unusual strain of the climb, I dropped quietly into the sand *outside* the Lingis camp and left it with no regret.

10

I pushed myself that night, running hard through the relative coolness of the silvery desert. I wanted as much distance as possible between me and the mining camp before my absence was discovered. Even after the moon set, and the darkness was nearly absolute, I kept moving. Caution slowed my pace, but I had already outrun the desert's edge with the ground-hugging bushes that could trip the unsuspecting. Now there was only salty sand, spraying up behind me and settling soundlessly to the gently rolling ground. As long as I made allowance for the ups and downs, I kept up a reasonably good pace.

In fact, I felt rather confident and self-satisfied as I ran through the blackness. I was as sure of my direction as if I could see Eddarta in the distance.

That might be Markasset's "inner awareness", I speculated, my mind separating itself from the hypnotic, rhythmic motion of my body. *But he's never shown evidence of such a strong link to the All-Mind. More likely,* I thought, and a warmth not of the desert filled me, *it's a light compulsion from Tarani. Lonna would have reached her before nightfall, so she knows I'm on my way, and she's helping as much as she can. It doesn't feel quite like the compulsion she used in Eddarta to bring us back together—but then, the distance is much greater.*

The lady does have power, I thought. *Enough, I hope—no, I'm sure, because she said so—to keep Indomel's at bay. But I won't rest easy until I get the Ra'ira and Tarani away from Eddarta's corruption.*

I had to pause, and laugh at myself. *Until I get them away,* I thought. *That's a good sign. I'm beginning to feel powerful again, myself.*

That good feeling sank a little the next morning, when something called my attention into the sky. I could barely see the small, gray-green bird against the grayness of the cloud cover, but I knew the maufa was on its way to Eddarta, with Tullen's trouble-making report in tow. I don't know whether the maufa or I was more astonished when a piercing shriek sounded and a huge white bullet dropped down from the clouds. The white shape collided with the green one, its straight course zigzagging with the impact; then wide wings opened and the two birds drifted down. Lonna dropped the maufa at my feet and hooted at me. I gripped my forearms and held them out; she settled into the square nest and lay her head across my shoulder.

I sat down, still holding her, and freed one arm to pick up the other bird, tiny in comparison to Lonna, its feathers stained with blood, its neck loose. *Why, Lonna*, I thought, *Why didn't you tell me you were a chicken hawk?*

"Tarani sent you, of course," I said aloud. "To gain time. No news to Indomel is good news. What's this you're carrying?"

When my hand felt the lumps under Lonna's wings, the big bird spread her wings and hopped out of my grasp. Tied to her sides, beneath and behind her wings where they wouldn't put direct strain on her powerful breast muscles, were two hand-size pieces of leather, not quite flat. I cut the lacings which held them, and they plopped into the sand, changing shape.

"Water!" I said, picking them up. They were small water bags made of specially treated glith skins. Tarani had put only a small amount of water in each one, out of consideration for the bulk and weight of Lonna's burden. But what she had sent nearly tripled my water supply.

"Tarani, Lonna—thank you," I whispered to the desert.

Lonna stayed with me for three days, feeding on the maufa she killed and flying off in the evenings to find her own water source. Following this straight desert route, the trip back to Eddarta was slightly shorter, but even more boring. I rejoiced when I caught a glimpse of color against the even grayness of the desert.

Eddarta was no exception to the one rule of landscape in Gandalara: where there was water, there also was abundant life; where no water flowed, "life" was brief, very chancy, and preferred night to day. That glimpse of color—nothing more, really, than a change from the gray scrubby bushes that clung to the sand to a greener variety—told me that the city was close.

On the trip from Eddarta, the troop had followed the River

Wall out of Eddarta, marching along gentle slopes at the base of the long, sloping wall. Near the city—and the lifegiving waters of the Tashal—those slopes had been thick with crops. From the crest of a hill, we had been able to see patterns to the land, smooth geometric shapes that changed color as the crops varied made use of every accessible square inch of irrigated land.

We had quickly left the farms behind us, but for miles beyond them, the land had continued to enjoy the rich base of groundwater supplied by the broad cascade of the Tashal and its myriad branches. The terrain had been wild and overgrown; without the smooth, winding line of road, it would have been slow going. It had reminded me of the terrain near Thagorn, except that here the uncultivated dakathrenil trees, their woody trunks twisting about only inches above the ground, were mixed with the slim but straighter, coniferous-looking trees I had seen planted in orchards near Dyskornis.

Walking through the one had brought back memories of riding through the other—which had led inevitably to the precious memory of the first time Keeshah's mind, and not merely his thoughts, had touched me. I had been embroiled in a fight with two Sharith, and keeping Keeshah out of it had been an essential element of my disguise—had they seen him, they would have known me as Markasset. So Keeshah had joined me in the only way he could—through our mindlink. His consciousness had merged with mine, providing instant interpretation of sounds and sights and scents that Markasset could not have processed so quickly, helping me win. Then—again for the sake of disguise—he had allowed me to ride the sha'um of the other men.

The memory had been with me constantly on that march, alternately a comfort and a torment, as the reality of Keeshah's absence pierced my reverie. I was just as glad now, as I stopped and let my panting slow, that I was approaching Eddarta from just this angle. I had missed that woody area, which had climbed the rolling upward slope of the River Wall and covered a narrow strip of level ground at its base. And I was too close to the wall to meet the treacherous salt bog that was the terminus for every surface water source in Gandalara— that, too, would have brought memories of Keeshah and our first trip together, out of the Kapiral Desert toward Raithskar. I was approaching Eddarta from the east, entering the cultivated area through an interface of scrubby bushes whose only differentiation from the desert growth was the healthier-looking green of their spiked leaves.

I called Lonna to ground, opened my pack, and wrote a brief note to Tarani. I tied the note to the bird's leg, and sent her off with Tarani's name as directions. Then I dug out a hollow in the sand in the scant shade of one of the bushes and settled in to wait.

It was dark when Lonna returned, and her call of welcome woke me from a deep sleep. It had been the first time in recent memory that I hadn't been troubled with restless dreams of unfilled needs and unanswered questions—whether that meant that the prospect of seeing Tarani had set them at rest, or merely that exhaustion had given me peace, I couldn't say.

The message Lonna carried was brief:

Lord City gate, midnight. tomorrow I will come to you. T.

The packet also contained a few small coins—a thoughtful addition, since I didn't dare try to change the gold pieces I carried. They displayed the countenance of Pylomel, the former High Lord, and had been minted some twenty or so years ago in honor of his planned marriage to Zefra. His plans had been delayed for two years, during which time Zefra had left Eddarta with Volitar, had given birth to Tarani (who had thought Volitar her father until recently) and had been, finally, captured and returned to Pylomel. The memorial gold coins hidden in my belt were rare enough to invite attention— the last thing I needed. The coins Tarani had provided were small in amount, but precious in their usability.

A small doubt crossed my mind, brought on by the realization that it was not only the dimness of light, and the flowing angles of Gandalaran cursive that made the note difficult to read. The words had been written in haste, and for a moment I wasn't absolutely positive that it was Tarani's handwriting.

Lonna was resting on my shoulder. I stretched out my arm and she side-stepped along it until her weight rested on my upper arm. "Did this message come from Tarani, Lonna?" I asked. She hunched forward and spread her wings; I laughed, and tossed her into the air. The big wings beat down, lifting her. "I see you haven't forgotten your stage training," I said, as she circled around my head and settled again on my shoulder. I stroked the feathers on her breast as I walked along. Your word is good enough for me, lady. Let's go find Tarani."

While I had moonlight, I walked on through the bushes and into farm land. I rested, then moved on at dawn. Midmorning I struck one of the wide roads that followed branches of the Tashal River, and led into Eddarta.

The city had no perimeter wall, but looked from a distance as though a giant hand had shaken buildings in a cup, like dice, then cast them in an untidy spill across the lowest slopes of the River Wall. From the time I stepped onto the road—and I knew it was my only choice, since sneaking around would only draw attention to myself—the skin on my back and neck prickled with the expectation of swordpoints behind me. I reached the outskirts of the city at noon, found myself a mediocre inn, had a mediocre meal that tasted like ambrosia after the hard, dried fruit and meat I had taken into the desert with me, and collapsed into a mediocre pallet for a sound eight hours of sleep.

I woke in the darkness of deep night, my "inner awareness" telling me that midnight was a good two hours away. I was alone in a second-floor room, and slightly amazed that I had rested so well.

I can think of several reasons, I thought to myself while I dressed, *why I shouldn't have slept a wink last night. Uncertainty whether Indomel knows I've left the Lingis mine, that just-before-action surge I've felt before when I got close to the Ra'ira, and—certainly not least of all—eagerness to see Tarani again. So why did I just check in here without thinking twice about anything, and pass out?*

Exhaustion has to be part of the answer, I finally decided. *But there's more.* I felt my teeth clench as I speculated. It was Ricardo who found the answer, in a memory from my early days in the Marines, when I'd been a well-trained but green kid on a soggy, enemy-infested island.

It's because I'm not giving the orders any more, I realized. *Tarani said escape, so I did. She said meet her at midnight, when I got here I had time to kill, so I caught up on my rest. It's kind of the reverse of Ricardo's wartime experience on Pelihau—when I got there, I was a buck private and I slept the sleep of the dead; when I left, I'd been promoted to Sergeant Carillo by default, and I'd learned to go for days without sleep.*

73

I shrugged. *She's the only one who's in a position to know what's going on*, I admitted, then felt a twinge of the guilt that still hovered at the back of my mind. *And she kept us on track while I was nonfunctional. We're a team*, I reminded myself. *Getting the Ra'ira out of Eddarta is the only thing that counts.*

I slipped the baldric over my shoulder, and touched the hilt of the bronze sword. *The Ra'ira—and Rika, if possible*, I thought, remembering the sight of Obilin holding the steel sword.

The city was quiet as I left the inn. The caution I had lacked on arrival here had claimed me again—the fewer people who saw me in Eddarta, the better.

At the edge of lower Eddarta, I paused to look up the wide avenue at Lord City. Crossing the desert seemed a snap, compared to walking up that paved, nearly empty road. To my right was the freshness and the rumble of the last fall of the Tashal cataract. It was visible only as a deeper darkness with an occasional spark of glimmering wetness. It called up the memory, once more, of our breakneck escape from the place I was now going.

I shuddered. *I hope this is the last time I go into Lord City*, I said to myself fervently. *This place is unhealthy in more than one way.*

I considered going east, out of the city, and trying to approach the gate more circumspectly than marching up the entry avenue. *No*, I decided. *That would probably draw more attention than my just walking up to the front door as if I had good sense and urgent business.*

So I gathered my determination, squared my shoulders, and started up the road. By the time I was approaching the wide, guarded gate, the skin between my shoulder blades was itching and crawling.

Markasset was used to enemies you could see, I thought, *and Ricardo certainly preferred them to hidden ones.*

There were two guards at the gate—standing, not leaning on the stone. Oil lamps set into the wall created a circle of wavering light. Visible through the open archway were spots of light from the short pillars that lined the walk to Lord Hall. All of those lamps had been lit on the night of the Celebration Dance. Only a few glimmered now in the darkness.

And something moved through the uncertain light, coming toward the gate, a darkness visible only when it blocked a lamp. It stopped a few feet inside the city; the guards had their backs to it, and it had made no sound at all. The shape was tall and slim, and I recognized it.

We're sitting ducks, both *of us!* I thought frantically. Panicky and confused, I stopped my approach to the gate, unsure whether I was to go in or she would come out.

I stopped.

My *legs* kept on walking.

11

It wasn't the first time I had felt a compulsion, but the experience was unnerving. Never mind walking boldly between two guards who probably had orders to kill me on sight—but who failed to see me. Discount the eerie setting, with the pale sky, the muttering of the river, the unsteady light, the oppressive sense of danger. What really spooked me was the ease of transition, and the strength of the compulsion. One minute I was walking on my own. The next second, someone else was doing the steering.

I had a wild suspicion, suddenly, that the tall figure might be Indomel, and not Tarani—but that fear, at least, was quickly put to rest. When I could see Tarani clearly, I saw lines of tension around her mouth and across her brow. She was dressed for desert travel in dark-toned trousers and thigh-length tunic. She didn't speak, but took my hand, turning with me to move toward Lord Hall and the walkway which led into the Harthim section of the miniature city.

I didn't speak, either—because I couldn't. I couldn't even tighten my hand around hers in a small gesture of greeting. The compulsion lay on my mind like a weight, numbing everything remotely related to muscular volition, while I walked beside Tarani into Lord City.

We passed a couple of people near Lord Hall, and there were more guards at the entrance to the Harthim living area. No one took any notice of us. Tarani led me through the back door of the maze of halls and stairways that had been built by generation upon generation of High Lords. We followed a route I had traveled once before, but I doubt I could have gone so unerringly to Zefra's quarters, had Tarani not been with me. As before, there were two guards beside the door. It had been left unlatched; Tarani pushed it open and we slipped through it; she shut it behind us.

The sound of door meeting frame, soft as it was, seemed a signal. The compulsion left me abruptly, and it seemed to take with it every ounce of my physical strength. I groped for the arm of a chair and sank into it.

I felt as if every nerve in my body was vibrating. It wasn't painful, but it wasn't pleasant. It was like the throbbing in a leg that was "waking" after having gone to sleep. I waited for the tingling to escalate into pain, but instead it only subsided, gradually, like water settling to smoothness after a disturbance.

When the sensation was gone altogether, I looked over at Tarani. She was seated in the chair next to me. Glass-chimneyed candles—Gandalaran lamps—gave the narrow, windowless anteroom a brightness that might have been cheery, with the knowledge of a bright day outside to boost the feeling. But it was the middle of the night, and my mood was far from cheery.

When Tarani saw that I had recovered from the effects of her compulsion, she reached across the gap between our chairs. Her smile faded as she looked at my face, and her hand drew back before it touched my arm.

"I am glad to see you safe," she said, her voice betraying her uncertainty.

"Safe from the *mines*," I said, not even trying to hide my anger. "But apparently not from you."

"From me?" she asked. "What have you to fear from me?"

"Control of my own mind," I snapped. I pushed myself up in the chair and leaned toward her. "After crossing half the world to get here, did you think I wouldn't follow you into Lord City willingly?"

"The compulsion?" she asked, and seemed truly surprised that I objected. "But surely you see that was the simplest, quickest way? Taking the time to explain would have been a ludicrous risk."

"To bring me through the gate, yes," I agreed. "But after that? No speech, no greeting, you just literally grabbed me, mind and body, and dragged me where you wanted to go."

Her eyes flashed, not with power but with anger. "And is this not where you wished to go, also?" she demanded.

"Yes, but *as my own choice*," I answered, slapping the arm of the chair.

She stood up and paced to the end of the small room, her arms crossed, the long-fingered hands gripping her shoulders. "Silence was absolutely necessary," she said with her back turned to me. "I was casting a difficult illusion to keep us from being seen. Any sound would have given us away."

77

"It didn't occur to you that I might figure that out on my own, and cooperate?" I asked bitterly.

"An illusion requires intense concentration," she said, her head bowed. "I thought, if you were free, you might wish to . . ." She faltered, then resumed in a steady, brisk voice. "To greet me in a way that would destroy that concentration. Perhaps I made a mistake in thinking that such a desire might overcome your sense of caution. Perhaps . . . no, truly," she said, turning to face me and throwing back her shoulders, "I knew that the danger I feared would have been real, had I been in your place and you in mine. It *was* foolish of me. No one knows better than I that you are always more mindful of duty than of anything else."

It was a sarcastic remark, calculated to sting, and it hit home.

"I keep forgetting," I said, standing up, "how good you are at illusion. You had me believing that you didn't blame me for our getting hauled back here."

"Why should *I* blame you," she flared, "when *you* were spending so much energy blaming yourself? And *our* presence here is a small inconvenience compared to the Ra'ira being within Indomel's reach."

"Small inconvenience?" I demanded. "Were *you* hauled off to the copper mines? Have *you* spent the last four days in the desert, plagued by worry about what you'd left behind and what you'd find in Eddarta?"

The heat of the argument had brought us closer together physically. We were within arm's length of each other when she said: "Were you not just speaking of trust? I sent Lonna with water and money, and she destroyed the message birds. Could you not believe, with that as evidence, that I would see to your safety in the city, as well?"

I grabbed her shoulders; she flinched at my grip. "It wasn't *my* safety that concerned me," I nearly shouted.

Her hands had caught my forearms. For a fraction of a second, I felt upward pressure, as she started to break my hold. But in that brief pause, I saw reflected in her face a thought that paralleled my own: *If I care so much for this woman, why am I yelling at her?*

The pressure ceased; her fingers lay lightly on my arms. I could feel their warmth through the fabric of the tunic.

"I was afraid for you, as well," she said, so quietly that I could barely hear her.

I kissed her.

It was worth a four-day trek across the desert.

I continued to hold her close to me, and she made no effort to move away.

"I'm sorry, Tarani. For getting us into this. For seeming not to appreciate your help. Believe me, that letter from you was like a waterfall in the desert. You've been doing the thinking for us for a while, and doing it well." I pulled away a little, lifted her chin to look into her face. "I promise you, I'm back on the team—all the way back."

That's as true, I thought, *as it can be. Keeshah has a part of me with him—but even if the "team" still included him, that part of me would be committed not to the team, but to Keeshah.*

My guts seized up with the sense of loss that was no easier to bear because it was familiar by now. I fought off the sensation and said: "Let's get the Ra'ira and leave Eddarta behind us for good."

Tarani hesitated, and I felt my calming paranoia re-activate itself. Seemingly undirected by rational thought, the space between us grew until we were again at arm's length.

"You did say in your letter that you and Zefra have found a way . . ."

"*to defeat Indomel*," she finished, after a brief pause. "But it is not so simple a task as defeating Gharlas, who was truly no more than a thief."

"Indomel," I said slowly, trying to keep my voice steady through the wave of savage eagerness that accompanied the thought, "will bleed like any other man."

"I said 'defeat'," she snapped, "not 'kill'."

"Why not?" I demanded. "Because he's your brother?"

"No—because he is the High Lord."

"So was your father the High Lord, but you didn't seem to regret his loss," I said.

"Neither," she said angrily, "did I wish his death. If you recall the circumstances, Thymas moved too quickly to give me any opportunity to make a choice."

"And would you have chosen to let him live?" I asked. "After the tortured life he had forced on you and Volitar?"

"I would choose to grant life to any man rather than demand his death," she said, straightening her shoulders.

79

The gesture seemed to be conscious, and it was a clue to something; part of my mind grabbed hold of it and started tracing a logic path, working beneath and in spite of the emotional turmoil that was dominating my reactions.

"I suppose that *is* true," I said, recognizing but helpless— no, unwilling—to control a nasty streak that surfaced now and then. "If you'd let Molik live, then any man could expect your mercy. And you can afford the appearance of generous intentions when you know that someone else will do your killing for you."

The first thing to register from the blow was surprise, then shock, then the stinging pain in the skin of my left cheek. My body reacted faster than my mind; I reeled back from Tarani's slap and then raised my hand to retaliate.

She faced me without flinching, but there was more pain in her face than anger.

I held back.

Molik's name did it, I thought. *That bastard's memory still has the power to shame her. When we were here before, she wouldn't even tell Zefra . . .*

My God, what have I done?

As soon as that logic, memory, and realization flashed through my mind—it took only an instant—I tried to lower my hand.

I couldn't.

In fact, now that I applied conscious effort to things outside my argument with Tarani, I realized there were several things I couldn't do.

Like . . . move . . . speak . . . breathe.

I must have been capable of some movement, because Tarani, looking straight into my face, had to be able to read my growing panic. She whirled away from me; from the corner of my eye I could see the inner door opening and Zefra stepping through.

"Release him, Mother!" Tarani ordered.

"He tried to hurt you." Zefra said in a low voice. "I have said it before, Tarani—you do not need this man."

Gharlas couldn't hold me in compulsion, I thought, mentally gritting my teeth and pushing back against the weight that had taken me over completely, with the same quickness that had unnerved me at the city gate. Zefra gasped with surprise.

"He is fighting me," she told Tarani. "Such a strong mind, so . . . different." She put her hands to her head, as though to shelter her eyes from a light too bright. "What is it, daughter? This man is too strange..." She looked at Tarani. "You have lied to me about him. Who is he?"

"He will be no one at all if you do not..."

"His death will be your doing, Tarani. Tell me who he is!"

I had been watching this with less interest as the struggle to free myself and the pressing need for air in my lungs consumed my attention. But I did see Tarani draw herself up—and again the gesture rang a bell—directly between her mother and me.

"And you have forced me to this," the girl said quietly. Suddenly she was with me, as she had been against Gharlas, and together we resisted Zefra's paralyzing compulsion. It was different this time. Then I had called up that part of me which had been Ricardo by concentrating on memories unique to a world two-thirds covered with water. But *then* the compulsion had been less severe, restricting only voluntary movement. Here there was no time. Tarani and I both pushed as hard as we could.

Zefra stepped back as if physically threatened, her arms straight in front of her. "No—oh!" She backed into the door, stood there for a moment as if pinned to it, then collapsed, sliding down to sit in a huddle on the floor. At that same moment, the compulsion let go; my body jerked, and I had to scramble to keep my balance.

Tarani knelt by her mother, reached for her arms, hesitated when Zefra flinched away from her, then persisted until she was holding her mother's upper arms and helping her to a chair. When Zefra was comfortable physically—her daughter turning against her, and proving to be more powerful was a shock from which she would recover slowly, if at all—Tarani stood up and came to me.

I forced myself to meet her eyes as I said: "I wouldn't have hit you."

To my great relief, she nodded. "I know," she said. "I saw it in your face in the instant *before* Mother..." She closed her eyes and said: "I am shamed that I struck you, Rikardon."

"I understand, Tarani—it wasn't me you wanted to hurt."

It was her turn to look relieved, then puzzled. "Why can it not always be like this between us, Rikardon? I do not need your words to tell me your meaning, and I feel it is the same for you."

"The Ra'ira," Zefra whispered.

Tarani turned as her mother stood up from the chair and came, walking a little shakily yet, toward us.

"You are near it here," Zefra continued. "And you are using it to see his thoughts. Do you need more proof, daughter, that you are fated to be the High Lord?"

All the clues clicked into place, and I groaned under the revelation. "That's what you meant by *defeating Indomel*, isn't it?" I demanded. "I don't know why I didn't catch on sooner. When you said that about not demanding anyone's life—that smacked of official policy, not just personal opinion."

I felt the anger kindle again.

"You're not planning to get the Ra'ira and go home, are you?" I demanded. "You're planning a fleabitten *war* between you and your brother!"

Tarani glared at me for a few tense seconds, then shrugged and laughed. "Thank you, Rikardon," she said, then spoke to Zefra.

"We are *still* near the Ra'ira, mother. And the silent understanding has faded." She sighed, and smiled at me almost shyly. "It is nothing of power," she said, seeming to speak more to herself than to either one of us. "And it will return. That knowledge makes the time between easier to bear."

I smiled back at her, feeling the sweetness start to grow again. "It was you who first told me that I say things I don't mean, Tarani. I've done a lot of that since I got here. I'm sorry."

"I, too, am at fault," she said. "Though I did not lie to you in my letter, I see now that I chose not to be truthful, for fear you would misjudge my motive.

"I give you my word, my love, that I still wish only to make the Ra'ira safe from Indomel. But the gem is actively and heavily guarded, though the guards have no idea what Indomel's prized treasure really is. I have considered every conceivable plan to get the stone back—yes, even to assassinating Indomel—and there is nothing that can be done, especially in the time left to us."

"'Time left to us'?" I repeated.

"The High Lord grows impatient for my 'help' to prove fruitful," Tarani answered. "He chafes at the lack of news from Lingis, and has sent special messengers to verify your presence. Once he learns you are gone, my 'privileged' position will vanish."

"What about your mindpower?" I asked. "Both of you, working together..."

"*Might* be able to control him," Tarani said. "Zefra did once, but only for a short time. He is strong, and alert to a compulsion attack from me. It would be too risky to gamble on making *him* get the Ra'ira for us."

"A direct victory is impossible," Zefra chimed in eagerly. "The only way for Tarani to get the Ra'ira is to *inherit* it—as the next High Lord."

"I thought you said you'd considered killing Indomel and rejected the plan," I said.

"We did," Tarani answered. "But that's the wrong way to go about it."

"No, it's better for Tarani to win her place in orderly fashion," Zefra said, pride and a well-remembered fanaticism bringing luster to her face and throat.

It was strange and unsettling to see someone so like Tarani in appearance and yet so different. The mindgift gave them both a look that set them apart from "normal" Gandalarans, but in Zefra that distinctiveness was somehow off-center, unwholesome.

"I can prove her birthright," Zefra continued, "and Tarani can prove her power. But to challenge Indomel empty-handed would be to invite disaster."

"Empty-handed," I mused. "Meaning, I suppose, that Indomel could produce the Ra'ira as confirmation of his right to rule?"

"Exactly," Zefra said, nodding. "The Lords know nothing about its powers, only its history. If Indomel has it, no matter how he got it, they will grant him his place."

"Are you saying that they *don't* know he has it?"

"He has told no one," Zefra said. "Of that I am absolutely sure. It would suit his style to wield a hidden power, and that may be why he keeps it locked away."

"It could also be," Tarani put in, "that he wishes to wait until he can use it easily before revealing it."

"Either way," I said, "he *has* it, which seems to be the deciding factor. Are you telling me that we're finished, that there's no way to get at him?"

"No—oh, no!" Zefra said. "The Ra'ira is a thing of legend, a *token* of personal power. Indomel might show it as a symbol, but he would never reveal its hidden qualities. Tarani need only present the assembled Lords with herself, her mindpower, and a symbol equally old and respected, and the Lords will acclaim her."

I reached into Markasset's memory and searched around. "There is nothing that will meet that need," I said at last, "no talisman of power that will rival the Ra'ira."

"There is," Zefra whispered. "A sword. Ancient. Made of rakor. It has the power Tarani needs."

Rakor was the Gandalaran word for steel.

"Rika," I said, and seemed to feel the weight of the sword in my hand. "We'll have to take out Obilin to get it back—and *that's* a plan I don't mind at all."

"How did Obilin get the Sharith's sword?" Zefra asked, surprised.

That's right, Thymas still had it when Zefra saw us in the Council Chamber, I recalled.

"The tale is too long for telling now, Mother," Tarani said, dismissing the subject.

"Rika will not do," Tarani said to me. "Serkajon's sword is a negative symbol to Eddarta. It speaks of treachery and defeat. And an attack on Obilin would be as fruitless and dangerous, while we are inside Lord City, as trying to steal the Ra'ira."

"There is another sword," Zefra said, warming to the discussion again. "As ancient as Rika—its twin, in fact. The swords were a pair, a treasure given to one of the Kings. He presented one to the Captain of the Sharith and kept the other, saying that they would be a symbol of the loyalty shared by King and Captain."

"*Another* steel sword?" I asked, reaching into Markasset's memory and finding absolutely no record of such a thing. As far as he had known, Rika was unique in iron-scarce Gandalara. "Supposing it *does* exist," I said, not caring that Zefra looked offended, "where is it now?"

Zefra answered stiffly. "When Serkajon betrayed Harthim, the Last King discarded the sword. He threw it from him violently, the stories say, all the while raging at the disloyal Captain. At the exodus from the capital, someone went to retrieve it, but Harthim ordered that it should lie where it had fallen, that its shame should be covered with dust."

I closed my eyes and counted to ten. It didn't help.

"It's in Kä, isn't it?" I asked. "All we have to do is find a city that's been lost for centuries, right?"

Both women nodded and smiled as if I'd just won a sixth-grade spelling bee. With one voice, they echoed the name: "Kä."

12

I took a step back from the two women. "Are you crazy?" I said.

Zefra's jaw tensed and her eyes narrowed. "Many in Eddarta believe so," Zefra said. "Take care you do not make the same error."

"Why don't you convince me, then," I demanded, "why it makes sense to go clear across the world in pursuit of something we may not find, when we *know* that something we could *use* is right here in Eddarta?"

"Because," Tarani said patiently, "those things are just as inaccessible here, and an attempt to get them is fraught with personal danger for all three of us."

"All we know about the location of Kä is that it's somewhere in the Kapiral Desert. Are you trying to tell me that there's no danger in marching out there with no idea where we're going—assuming, of course, that we get away from here with our skins and walk clear across the world *before* we start looking?"

Tarani's patience was wearing thin. "Do you hear what you are saying, Rikardon? 'March' into the desert. 'Walk' across the world. I think that you do not object to the plan as much as to the discomfort of making the search on foot. The Sharith are few, my friend; the rest of us must walk wherever we wish to go. Yet few people of any sense have died in the Kapiral or any other desert."

"Sharith?" Zefra asked; we both ignored her.

I hate to admit it, I thought, *but she may be right. Looking for that stupid city seems a much bigger job without Keeshah. Maybe I'm even afraid . . .*

"Everyone *else* has learned those survival skills," I said slowly. "I have never needed them."

"Then how did we survive *walking* through the Chizan Passage?" Tarani demanded. "And that terrible crossing from

Sulis to Stomestad, with an injured man and a sha'um who *slowed* our movement?"

I said what I felt, though I knew it had little logic. "Keeshah was *there*, Tarani. It's different, now."

She put her hand on my shoulder, a welcome tenderness in the gesture. "Keeshah is *not* the source of your strength, my love. How did you get to Eddarta?" she asked.

"I . . . ran," I answered.

"The route?" she demanded.

"Across desert," I answered, seeing her point but still fighting it. "But Lonna . . ."

"Lonna will be with us in the Kapiral, as well," Tarani said. "If necessary, she will bring food, as well as water. We *can* do this, Rikardon. And we must. It truly is the only way we can be sure Indomel never abuses the power of the Ra'ira."

I sighed. "You still haven't told me how you expect to find the city," I said.

"Tarani's link with the All-Mind is very strong," Zefra said. "She read the Bronze; she will be able to find Kä." Zefra moved forward, pressed herself between her daughter and me. "Tarani could do it *alone*," she said, and turned her back to me.

"Who is this man, daughter?"

"He, not I," Tarani said calmly, "is the key to finding Kä."

"*What?*" Zefra said, beating me to it by only a fraction of a second.

"In body, he is the last of Serkajon's line," Tarani began.

Zefra gasped and interrupted. "That traitor—" I tensed for the attack that was telegraphed in her voice, but Tarani grabbed her mother's shoulders and held her facing away from me.

"In body *only*, Mother. He is a Visitor. I am convinced that he comes from the time of Kä, from among the Sharith *before* the end of the kingdom. I—" She glanced over Zefra's shoulder at my face, which must have registered the astonishment I felt. "I have not even told *him* this, Mother, but I believe he has come to bring the Kings and the Sharith back together. Why else would he have been proclaimed Captain of the Sharith?"

Another gasp from Zefra.

"And the first steel sword, the one Obilin now has, that sword belongs to him. Don't you see, the swords are the symbol of the betrayal of the Sharith. Rikardon is meant to re-unite them. *He* will find the other one."

"It does not belong to him!" Zefra cried. "It is yours by right!"

"It shall be mine, Mother. And when we return here, defeat Indomel and reclaim *his* sword from Obilin, then Rikardon and I, as leaders of the Sharith and the Lords, will set the pattern for the future. As we shall be together, so shall those who follow us."

No, I looked over Zefra's shoulder at Tarani's flushed and earnest face, and my chest tightened until it threatened to stop my lungs. *Oh, no. This place has contaminated her—that "absolute power" nonsense, except it isn't nonsense. How long has Tarani been here? Five weeks? Six? All it took was for Tarani to learn that her mindpower is especially strong, and that she's legally—if that word has any application in this contorted society—in line for political power, and she's convinced herself that she can "save" the Ra'ira by getting it for herself.*

Zefra glanced over her shoulder at me, then sighed and turned back to her daughter. "I must trust your choice in this, Tarani, but I cannot hide my doubts. It may not be as I fear, that he will try to turn you from your purpose. But take care that your feelings for him do not challenge your commitment to Eddarta, to the Ra'ira . . . to me."

In other words, I thought grimly, *don't let the s-o-b get in the way of your rise to power*. The chest tightness was still with me, allowing me barely to breathe. I made a conscious effort to relax. *Don't panic*, I warned myself. *We'll soon be away from Zefra. If Tarani was so easily swayed into Zefra's thinking patterns, maybe she'll swing the other way as easily. Zefra may even have used a little subtle compulsion on Tarani.* The thought was hopeful—because it made Tarani's new direction less threatening—and frightening, because it led the way to another discovery. The tightness in my chest wasn't fear or grief; it was Tarani's doing.

Another compulsion. I'm damned if she can just do this to me whenever she feels like it, I thought furiously.

Grimly, I fought back.

Tarani gasped, moved restlessly, then pulled her mother into her arms. "We must go now, Mother," she said, looking straight at me, her eyes shining in the lamp light. "We'll be back. Care for yourself well."

Zefra turned to me, and the compulsion clamped down. I stood there, outwardly immobile, seething inside, while Zefra stared at me.

"What I have said of you, Rikardon—I am Tarani's mother. If you both return here safely, I will offer my apology, and you will share the love I bear my daughter." Her voice thickened, and she drew herself up—at that moment, she was every inch a ruler, not a prisoner. "If anything happens to Tarani, however . . ."

"Nothing will happen, Mother," Tarani interrupted the threat. "We will both return, soon." She hugged her mother once more; I felt myself bow stiffly.

Tarani snatched up a few things that waited on the ledge at one side of the room: a water pouch, a baldric with sword and dagger, and a second pouch that jingled with coins. She slipped on the baldric hurriedly, then took my hand and led me to the hallway door, paused to open it slowly, and marched us out between the two guards.

We retraced our steps, a little less smoothly than before. I was fighting the compulsion, staggering, forcing Tarani to drag me along physically. There was a bitter satisfaction in the way she gasped for breath and pulled at our linked hands in uneven spurts of energy, but the contest was nonphysical. It wasn't even mental, except as the mind is supposed to be able to control the will. It was a conflict of desire, so strong that it took on some of the character of muscles flexing and opposing. It seemed to me that the purpose of the struggle had shifted. It wasn't that I wanted to voice my objections and she wanted me silent. It was much more basic than that. She wanted to control me, and I wanted to prove she couldn't.

When we approached the city gate, I stopped struggling. Tarani stopped pulling and we rested for a minute, while she quieted her own heavy panting. Such sounds might give us away to the guards when we got nearer. I could see Tarani's face clearly in the silvery moonlight, and she was looking at me with a mixture of curiosity and consternation.

What do you think? I asked her silently. *That I'd let this quarrel interfere with our escape? We may have different reasons but right now I want the same thing you do—to get the hell out of Lord City, Eddarta, and this part of the world.* The pressure of the compulsion lessened, but I could feel it poised, ready to clamp down again.

Tarani, if you have any skill at thought reading at all, hear this, I pleaded, not quite sure that she couldn't hear me. *Take away the compulsion. Show me that you have some trust left for me. Take it all away. Let's walk out of here side by side, partners again.*

The compulsion made itself felt again—tight, compelling. She turned toward the gate and took my hand, and *Tarani walked me out of Lord City.*

She held the compulsion until we were halfway down the ramped road to the larger city.

It was still nearly two hours before dawn, and the road was utterly deserted, the stones of its pavement glistening and slick from condensation. This road and the river branch that followed it closely on the west linked the two parts of Eddarta. The other side of the road—as well as the hillside on the opposite side of the river—was kept free of tall growth so that the Lord City guards could have clear view in every direction downslope from the walls of the city. The slopes weren't cultivated, but the nearness of so much water supported a lush carpet of ground cover that was sort of like the grass Ricardo had known, but taller, multiple-bladed, with fatter stalks.

It was onto this spongy, sweet-smelling carpet that Tarani and I tumbled, the moment she released her compulsion. I caught her off guard, jerked at her arm, and we rolled down the bank of the built-up roadbed into one of the hollows of the uneven slope.

It was a gesture of defiance and, I suppose, of revenge.

I was mad at *her* for not trusting me.

I was mad at *myself* for having lost her trust.

I was mad at *her* for letting Zefra twist her.

I was mad at *myself* for getting us recaptured and exposing her to Zefra's influence. I wasn't angry. I was *mad*, and determined to get some things straightened out, right then. Even though there was no one in sight, I felt exposed, standing on the moon-glittered stones of the road. So I pulled her off the road, not particularly gently, but with only the conscious goal of getting us to a place that felt more private.

The bank was steeper than it had seemed, and we rolled together as we fell. The muscles of her arm and back moved under my hands; her legs tangled with mine; her breasts cushioned my weight as I rolled over her. Clear and sharp as a whip snapping, I felt a different need unleashed in me, absorbing and overwhelming the fury that had started our fall. When we came to a halt, I sprawled full length on top of her, pressed my mouth against hers, and fumbled urgently with the hem of her tunic, groping for the tie that fastened her trousers.

I couldn't have imagined it. She was responding, arching against me, speaking wordlessly deep in her throat, her hands pressing thrills to my neck and back.

The whip snapped again, and she was fighting me. Her hands pushed against my shoulders. A leg that had caressed mine came between our bodies and braced against my hip. I pulled at it, dislodged it, pressed against her. Her forearm slammed the side of my head, sending a blinding flash of pain to my cheek and jaw—and she was free. She scrambled away and crouched, watching me, waiting for the next attack.

It was that posture that brought me to my senses. It wasn't the stance of a woman terrified of a rapist. There was nothing of desperation, even of fear, in the way she looked at me. She was a fighter defying her enemy, challenging him, eagerly awaiting the next encounter.

And I was the enemy.

The fury and the need drained out of me, leaving me weak. I took a deep breath and rubbed my face, ignoring the way my hands trembled. The skin on the left side of my face tingled, and my jaw felt tender.

I let myself drop to the ground. Tarani moved slightly to keep me directly in front of her, not relaxing her guard. *Come on*, I thought. *I wouldn't blame you if you flayed me alive*. I was empty of words. I couldn't explain what had happened, even to myself. How could I hope to ask her forgiveness?

So I sat silently, waiting for her to decide what to do, ready for whatever action she wanted to take.

She laughed.

It was the first coherent sound either one of us had made, and it wasn't the lovely sound I remembered. It was harsh, triumphant, shocking in the silent night. So shocking, in fact, that it even surprised her. It broke off abruptly and she looked around, as if wondering where the sound had come from. Her gaze rested on me, and she seemed to melt down into a little ball, huddled against the opposite slope of the small hollow.

It seemed like hours that we sat there, struggling—I, at least—to comprehend what had happened. Yet my inner awareness told me it was only a few minutes later that Tarani stirred. I sat up, too, and braced myself. I was ready for what she would say—I had lived it over and over again in those few minutes.

Tarani had approached me gently in the desert and I had refused her. By what right had I now tried to claim her by force? She *had* responded; of that I was sure. To my already guilty mind, that only made it worse. I was afraid that I had brutalized—and destroyed—her feelings for me.

I didn't say any of that; I expected her to say it. But she only stood up, stared at me for the briefest instant, dropped her gaze, and started the climb back to the road. I followed her and we walked, side by side but not touching, into larger Eddarta.

13

The city was wakening, getting ready for the day, but as yet there were few people moving about the streets, and soft echoes of our footfalls ghosted behind us. The city was built mostly of stone, reed, and brick, and it was old—older than any place Ricardo had seen in his own world. It showed its age in the patched roofs, where newly cut reed tops were dark splotches against the aged, bleached thatching. Nearly all the structures in larger Eddarta were two stories high; carefully fitted baked-clay bricks were strengthened with a mortar of dried mud. That, too, spoke in its multishaded patterns of years and years of repair.

In this pre-dawn quiet, the city seemed huge and empty. At midday, the streets teemed with crowds of people. Traders, searching out bargains. Lords, looking for particular objects or merely out slumming. Most of all, Eddartans, looking to purchase those things they couldn't produce themselves—butchers out to buy bread, a baker looking for a new suit, weavers in search of jewelry.

Eddarta shrank under the force of those crowds, but never gave Rikardon the claustrophobic feeling Ricardo had experienced in some of the older European cities he had visited. This city might be old, but it was still quite modern. In Gandalara, there was no iron-based technology to create a need for newness. *Old* and *obsolete* were not the equivalent terms in Gandalara that they sometimes were in the world Ricardo had known.

The streets of Eddarta, built for the foot passage of people, still served their purpose very well. Those areas of the city which permitted vleks and carts had been built with wider streets to accommodate the different sort of traffic, and those streets were still wide enough. It might be that the carts were better made now, but that was the only change in "modern" Eddarta.

It was down one of those wider streets that Tarani led me.

When we stopped in front of a door, I asked: "Is this Carn's shop?"

She nodded, not looking at me, and tapped lightly on the door, once, and then twice more.

Carn was the name of a man friendly to the Fa'aldu, part of the group which helped slaves escape. On our way to Eddarta the first time, Vasklar at Stomestad had given us Carn's name as someone to go to if we needed help.

The door opened into darkness and we slipped through it.

"Speak ye the word," growled a bass voice to our left. The windows were tightly covered with louvered shutters. As my eyes adjusted to the interior darkness, I could make out a slim shadow against one of the dimly glowing rectangles.

"To drink in the desert," I said, remembering the amusement with which I had heard Vasklar's solemn pronouncement of the "password". Having seen the mines, and having learned what escaping slaves risked if recaptured, I was no longer amused.

"That be an old word, my friends," the man said. "Name the one that gave it you."

"Vasklar," Tarani said. As the light grew with the outside dawn, details became clearer—like the dagger in the man's hand, turning restlessly from a thin black line to a triangular shadow. At the sound of our friend's name, he lowered the dagger and took a step backward.

"Aye, he said two might come. Another word, for surety—a name."

"A name?" Tarani said, confused—but I thought I knew what the man meant.

"Thymas," I said. "He was with us at Stomestad."

The dagger's shadow disappeared, and a strong-fingered hand closed on my arm. "A light not be safe as yet. What need ye? Have ye fed?"

"Sleep," Tarani murmured, and I thought of all she had gone through in the past few hours. Strangely, there was no anger associated with the thought of the compulsion she had held for so long, only awareness that it had required a great deal of energy to handle compulsion and illusion at the same time. Then the struggle—

My mind sheered away from thinking about that.

"We need a safe place to sleep," I said. "Then food, if you can spare it. Then—"

"It be enough for now," he stopped me. "Will ye be sought this day?"

"Aye," I said. "It be likely."

His dialect is easy to pick up, I thought, *even though this is the first time I've heard it. Come to think of it, the Gandaresh I've been exposed to is strikingly homogeneous. The Lords have a slightly more formal style, but for the most part, Gandalarans from both sides of the world speak nearly the same language. His syntax is different, as well as the inflection—I hope I'll have time to ask him about it.*

Carn went to the window, pulled a brace bar, and opened the shutter a crack. A bar of lighter gray spilled into the room, and by that slight illumination, Carn gestured to me for help. For the first time, I could see that this was not so much a room as a storehouse. Goods of different kinds were stacked against the interior walls, packed for travel in bone-handled nets. I saw cloth, and art pieces, and—a long bundle, wrapped in heavy cloth—the gleaming tip of a bronze sword.

A prism-shaped stack of rolled carpet stood away from the walls, in the center of the room. Carn had me lift one end of the top roll, exposing a hollow area protected by an inverted V of tied reeds. Then he started pulling away false ends, short rolls of carpet identical to matching rolls on the other side. In the few minutes we worked, the sliver of gray light had brightened until the entire room was visible. When I looked inside the tent of carpet we had opened, I could see a yawning blackness in the floor.

"'Tis not a large place," Carn said, breathing heavily, "but it be room enough for a day's rest. Use the lamp wisely; I'll stamp three times when it's time for ye to come out again. The end of this day, at least."

I brought Tarani from where she rested on a heap of fabric. In the new day's light, her weariness showed in the shadows under her eyes and the waxiness of her normally pale skin. Carn looked at her and caught his breath. I thought he might question us, but he merely said: "Aye, Lords will seek such a one."

I crawled through the triangular hollow to the floor opening and lowered myself gingerly to stand on an earthen surface, my shoulders above the room's brick-laid floor. Carn helped me pull Tarani's half-conscious form through the "doorway" in the tent of carpet. In stages, Tarani cooperating

94

as best her exhaustion would allow, I lifted her down through the cellar entry and carried her along a short, shallow ramp to a small room that barely allowed us to stand. I had only seconds to look around before Carn started replacing the carpet ends and shutting out what little light had followed us down. The walls were bare earth, like the floor, and one was sweating gently, creating at its base a small stream of water which leaked out of the room through its own fist-size tunnel.

I marked the placement of the lantern, appreciated the provision of a chamberpot and a water jug; then darkness set in. Tarani shivered, and so did I. It was the first time I could remember feeling physically cold in Gandalara, and I supposed it was the dampness and the nearness of the river.

I had glimpsed a pile of bedding in the nearest corner. I left Tarani momentarily, sorted out pallets from blankets by feel, and did the best I could to make us a bed. Sleep and warmth were too paramount for any consideration of propriety or embarrassment. I pulled Tarani close against me under the blankets. She huddled into the warmth, shivered violently once, and fell asleep with her arms tucked into my chest and her head on my shoulder.

I awoke to a vibration in the ground beneath and around me. The blankness and the dank smell of the place kept me disoriented for a second or two, then a pleasant ache in my arm recalled Tarani's presence and brought the situation into focus.

Must be people up above, I decided. Confirmation came immediately as voices filtered faintly through the cushion of carpet that enclosed the entrance to this place.

Tarani stirred. I eased away from her, yawning, and felt around for the lamp and the sparker, attached to the lamp base by a length of string. I gripped the scissor-like handles of the sparker and snapped the flint against the tiny piece of steel. The noise seemed unbearably loud in that small area, as did the hiss as the wick of the candle caught. But once the chimney was in place, casting refracted light all around us, some of the cold and fear leeched out of us. We could see one another, and the room.

Tarani reached out to touch the lamp chimney with shaking fingers. "The design—it's like—could it be that *he* made this?"

"Volitar?" I asked, thinking again that I would have liked to get to know the man who had been a father to Tarani. Once a

95

gemcutter, he had adopted a new trade late in his life, that of glassmaker. "Why not?" I shrugged. "It won't be the first coincidence we've run across."

Not by a long shot, I affirmed silently.

Tarani's hand dropped away from the lamp chimney. "For the first time," she said, "I am glad Volitar is dead. Glad that he did not live to see what Zefra has become . . . what she has been always."

She looked at my face, nodded to herself, and smiled bitterly.

"Yes, I see her clearly, Rikardon. In the days I have spent in Eddarta, she has talked of nothing but my 'rightful place' as High Lord. And in her speech I heard years of loneliness, helplessness, imprisonment, frustration. She is mad indeed, mad with a need for the power which has made her its victim." She sighed. "Nor can I fault her for it. I have shared her cell for only a few weeks, and—" Her voice shook. "And I am no longer confident of my own sanity."

She huddled into herself, the attitude of her body warning me away.

"You're thinking of—what happened on the hillside," I said. It didn't have to be a question.

"Yes," she said. Her voice came out choked, awkward. "I am sorry, Rikardon. I cannot tell you why . . . I mean, I did want . . . forgive me."

She's blaming herself? I thought, astounded. *After I attacked her, she's apologizing for not letting herself be raped?*

"There is nothing to forgive," I said. Shame overwhelmed me; I couldn't go on. Shame—and something else.

Thought of the hillside had brought forth a tactile memory of Tarani's body beneath me, and with memory came desire. I wanted Tarani again, with the same scary fierceness. I fought to control it, taking deep breaths, clenching my hands until my arms trembled.

Tarani saw my distress, and did exactly the wrong—or the right, depending on viewpoint—thing. She rocked up to her knees, leaned across the distance between us, and put her arms around my neck.

What little control I had, dissolved in that instant.

I kissed her roughly and swung her, beneath me, to the pallet-covered dirt floor. She struggled, pulled her face away, gasped for breath, beat at me with her hands. I pinned her wrists above her head and kissed her again, forcing her legs apart, pressing into the softness between them.

Caught up in need, I started pushing at her rhythmically, the two-layer cloth barrier a torment of frustration. I growled, shifted my grip so that one hand held both Tarani's wrists, and pulled awkwardly at her clothing.

She twisted her face away from mine and gasped: "Let go. Please. Let go." It was then I noticed that the rhythm wasn't mine alone. Her hips rose to meet me, her legs spreading wider with every thrust. "Please let go," she groaned again, and I released her wrists.

For a frantic few seconds, we struggled with the clothes, reluctant to break the haunting, building, compelling rhythm long enough to clear away the barriers. Then she had one leg free of her trousers, mine were pushed out of the way, and her softness opened to me.

We both cried out as I entered her. Tarani's hands gripped my neck, and her mouth sought mine as we moved together in sweet and scary excitement, wanting it to be over, wanting it never to end.

At the last, I broke away from her embrace, levered myself up on my arms, and focused every fiber of consciousness on the fused heat that was both of us, throbbing between her legs. Her hands slid down to my buttocks, gripped and relaxed, not so much guiding as amplifying the rhythm of our striking flesh, sending tremors of anticipation up my spine.

The moment came when we knew release was imminent. I moaned in joy and grief. Her pelvis twitched, creating a slightly different angle; her legs spread even wider. And, suddenly, I was pounding into the full, flattened softness, pounding and roaring and not hearing Tarani's scream of relief, and joy, and despair.

Tarani's labored breathing brought me back to the world. I heaved myself up on my elbows, and her lungs, relieved of pressure, gulped in air. She opened her eyes, and I knew that she, too, had only now wakened. Afraid to see what lay in her eyes, I kissed her gently.

Her lips were soft, responsive, eager. With a thrill of joy, I felt myself, still joined to her, begin to stiffen. Welcoming it, nurturing it, I let my lips touch her face, her throat. I slipped my hand under the fabric of her tunic and caressed her breast, full and firm. She moved and made a sound—and we took the time, then, to be free of all our clothing.

I kissed her breast and breathed her name: "Tarani".

She held my head against her and whispered back. "Ricardo. Oh, Rikardon."

What did she say? I thought—then lost interest.

We were in the grip of need once again, less urgent for its recent satisfaction, but no less strong. It built more slowly, climbed just as high, and left us, this time, exhausted and at peace. I had strength enough to roll my weight off Tarani. Still joined, we slept.

14

A stamping sound from above roused us, then we heard Carn's voice whispering from the opening. Light spilled down from the wide square, wavering and shivering.

Lamp light, I thought. *Can it be night again, so soon?*

"It be time to go," Carn's voice was saying in a projected whisper. "I've a meal for ye; I'll leave it here. Did ye hear?"

"Yes," I said, as Tarani stirred beside me. "We heard, Carn. Thank you."

"Aye," was all he said, and I heard his footsteps move away from the opening. He had left the light, which was a good thing. The candle in our lamp had burned itself out while we slept.

Tarani lay in the shadow of my body, so I couldn't see her face when she came fully awake. Neither could I miss the sudden tension in her body. We moved apart, felt around for our clothes. I pulled a tunic over my head, heard and felt it rip, and pulled it off again.

"I think this is yours," I said, holding it out toward the shape which was all I could see of her. It was lifted from my hand and another tunic left there. We sorted out our clothes and dressed, neither one of us suggesting that it would be easier with light.

I didn't know how Tarani was feeling, but I felt clear-headed for the first time in—days? weeks? Light-headed, too—whether from relief or lack of food, I couldn't say. I was a little shocked, definitely embarrassed by what had happened between us, but not regretful.

No, not at all regretful.

The memory of it stirred me in a distant, unreal way—because, in memory, I could leave behind the feeling, identifiable only now, that the need had been separate from us, an entity all its own, moving us, controlling us, using our bodies to satisfy itself. The force, the savagery of what Tarani and I

99

had shared had been wonderful, exalting... and terrifying. I had no desire to re-create it.

That was a once-only, I told myself, *the product of all our frustration on many levels, expressing itself in the most basic way possible. I think we both would have preferred something more gentle, but at least, now, the edge is off. Gentleness can come later, provided Tarani can cope with what happened. If we get out of this mess alive, Tarani,* I promised her silently as I watched her silhouette put on a final boot, *I'll give you all the time you need. Whatever you need. Anything is worth getting there again, both of us willing, both of us reaching for it with our hearts as well as our bodies.*

"Ready for dinner?" I asked her.

"Yes, I am hungry," she said, her voice subdued.

I almost reached for her, then, nearly overcome with tenderness.

You just promised to give her time, I reminded myself sharply, and threw myself toward the opening in the floor overhead. *She has to find her own answers.*

I brought down the lamp and the plate of fruit, meat, and bread, and went back for the pitcher of cool water. We ate in silence, awkwardly and separately availed ourselves of the chamberpot, then crept up the ramp and poked our heads out of the floor opening.

"Carn," I called out in a whisper.

"I be here," he answered, and stepped in front of the opening in the carpet. He was tall and lanky, with rounded shoulders and long, muscular arms. One eye and one side of his mouth drooped slightly, giving him a permanent, wry expression. "Best be ye hurry a bit," he said.

We crawled out into the storeroom; he stepped back to let us out, then turned away abruptly and walked toward the back of the room. "Leave the city by the second street," he said, referring to the system by which the oldest, main street had been supplemented on alternate sides by parallel avenues. "Ye'll be met at the joining by two who'll trade clothes wi' ye, and give ye instructions for where to join up with Tellor's caravan. Ye'll need to move quickly, mind."

We had made our way through the rear door of the room into a smaller room that seemed to serve as an office. Carn stopped by a woven-reed door on the opposite side of the room and turned back to us.

"'Tis a hurried job I've done for ye, but it be the best I

100

could do in shorttime. It be clear ye cannot stay in Eddarta..."
His voice trailed off, then he closed his mouth and turned
toward the door.

"And?" I prompted him. "You were going to say something
else?"

"'Tis naught," he said, but I caught his arm.

"I know you understand the risks you've taken to help us,
Carn," I said. "And there is little we can do to repay you.
Whatever is important to you is also important to us."

He looked up and shifted from foot to foot. At last he
dropped his eyes and said: "Indelicate it be, but hap it needs
saying." He rubbed his hand quickly over his face as if
scrubbing it. "The noises ye made," he said, all in a rush.
Tarani caught her breath, and I'm sure my neck began to
redden. "And not but me heard them, neither. Folk passing
in the street stopped in to ask of it."

"What—" I had to clear my throat. "What did you tell
them?"

Carn had caught the reason for my hesitation. "'Tis not a
jest!" he protested. "Seekers, watchers, might have heard!"
Then he flexed his shoulders back, and looked at me with the
start of a smile. "I spake that my wife was entertaining a Lord
upstairs, and a trick of the building made it seem the sounds
were below."

"Would your wife support that, if the Lords come questioning?" I asked.

Carn shrugged. "They were strangers who asked—why
should they care of my wife's honor? Nor am I wed, in any
case."

I laughed, reached out my right hand, and took his. He
responded with a warm grip, even though the gesture was
strange to him.

"Vasklar is expecting ye at Stomestad in two seven-days,"
he told us. "To hear the desert folk speak of ye, there is little
ye cannot do." He nodded at us, including both of us.

*The Fa'aldu would make great publicity agents in Ricardo's
world*, I thought. *They've managed to make me a legend
while frequently keeping me from becoming a dead one.*

"Keep ye well," Carn said. "Hap I shall hear news of ye
now and again."

We were out the door and down the street before I realized
that I had never asked him where he came from, how he had
acquired that odd accent.

There are some things I may never know about this world,
I told myself, and was a little surprised that the thought
wasn't frustrating. *The only thing better than having curiosity
satisfied is having more to be curious about,* I thought, not at
all sure I believed it.

It was early evening, and the center of the city would be
crowded, now, with people relaxing after the day's work.
There wasn't a district in this city for places such as I had
seen in Raithskar and Chizan—a gaming house, or what
Ricardo might have called a casino. But there were plenty of
"come have a drink" places that provided tables and game
pieces, should the customers want to play a friendly round of
mondea on their own. Those places, and the restaurants,
would be doing a booming business about now.

But Carn's storeroom was west and south of the main part
of the city. As nearly as I could judge it (considering the
stacks and stacks of various products I'd seen), Carn must
have been a caravan agent, someone who collected the goods
for a caravan master to pack and carry to other markets. It
was an ideal position for someone who was also an agent for
an escape route.

Eddarta wasn't guarded in the sense that everybody had to
step through a tollgate and display some identification. You
might say that everyone, consciously or unconsciously, guarded everyone else.

The Lords were not liked, but neither was Eddarta a rebel
city held under armed guard. The people were bound solidly
to their lives by tradition and familiarity, and viewed anyone
who turned his back on the system with a mixture of envy
and resentment—and sometimes greed. When Tarani and I
had entered Eddarta as the tailor, Yoman, and his daughter,
Rassa, one of Yoman's "friends" had already moved into his
house/shop.

There had to be a few Eddartans who, spotting a native
on his or her way out, would go straight to the appro-
priate landpatron and report or sell the information. Most
folks, though, simply noticed it and talked about it, and it
wouldn't be long before someone in Lord City heard the
news.

Tarani and I weren't natives, but neither were we totally
strangers. Enough people had seen us on the way *into*
Eddarta, surrounded by dralda and High Guard, that there
was a fair chance we could be recognized.

Caution demanded that we walk through the outskirts of the city boldly, make no attempt to disguise ourselves, and simply take our chances of being stopped before we met our contacts outside the city. The "joining", where the city avenues merged into a single wide road leading eastward, also marked a turning point of safety; past it, no extra light was provided. Until we reached it, however, we walked between waist-high brick pillars that held oil and slow-burning wicks. We couldn't be as clearly seen as in daylight, but neither did we feel as safe as we might have felt, had we been walking through a moon-grayed world under the pale night sky.

Tarani's power, while it seemed much stronger than before, still demanded a great deal of her energy—her fatigue when we had finally reached Carn testified to that. She didn't offer to disguise us, and I didn't ask it of her, because by any measure we had a rough trip ahead of us. She would need all her energy.

There's another factor, too, I thought. *We can't become dependent on her power.*

Physical disguise was out of the question. *Too bad the hooded cloak isn't fashionable in Gandalara,* I moaned. *I've only seen two kinds of hoods—the jeweled ones the ladies were wearing at the Celebration Dance and, if you could call them hoods, the desert scarfs.*

We carried such scarfs threaded through our belts, and there would have been little danger in wearing them in the normal style—that is, tied around our heads with the long point of the triangle dangling down our backs. Desert dress wasn't an uncommon sight on the outskirts of the city. But the scarf's protective arrangement, with the free end pulled around to cover most of the face, would attract too much attention here.

Skulking about, trying not to be seen, would also be an attention-getter for the inevitable few who *would* see us. So Tarani and I just walked at a comfortable pace through Eddarta and tried to project a "belonging" image.

There weren't many people on the road, and most of them were going our way—farmers who had brought in their produce and spent their day in the city shopping or drinking. There were more vleks than people, actually, and everybody looked downhearted and tired. Few Eddartans actively opposed the landpatron system. I had heard a lot of gripes, while free in the city when we'd been here before, about general conditions, but they had been largely undirected complaints, as though the people couldn't see that it was the Lords who sat at the center of their unhappiness.

And maybe that's not really true, I thought. *It's easy for an outsider to make quick judgments, and through both Ricardo and Markasset, I'm pre-conditioned to dislike this system.*

I considered that idea for a moment, and tried to put myself into the perspective of the classes of people I had encountered in Eddarta: a Lord, a landservant, and a slave.

Ah, it's no use, I thought. *My biases are too strong. I can't detect a shred of "human" dignity in any of those roles, especially in the Lords. They're parasites, skimming the wealth of this part of the world...*

Wait a minute. What makes them different from the major capitalists of Ricardo's world? I wondered. *The Rockefellers, the Duponts, the oil cartels—they "ruled" after a fashion. They dictated world economic conditions, the survival of rival businesses, the very lives of the people who depended on their products. Why don't I despise their memory as violently as I do the Lords?*

The All-Mind, I realized. *It's not just Markasset's memories I'm dealing with here, but the influence of generations of memory. Whether it's just memory, or really the surviving personalities of all Gandalarans, though, aren't Eddartans just as much a part of it as Raithskarians? So there ought to be considerable* support *within the All-Mind for the Eddartan system. Right?*

I let the problem filter into the corners of my mind and occupy all the places where worry had been hiding. A part of my mind, just before I descended into total preoccupation, recognized that I hadn't had the pleasure of this sort of intellectual exercise since Keeshah had left my mind in shock. The puzzles I had dealt with while trying to stay sane as Obilin's captive—those had been familiar. This was a new one, and I welcomed it.

Those in favor of the Lord system would probably be a minority, I figured, *but the Lords were born of the Kings, and the Kings had the support and confidence of the entire Gandalaran population for many, many generations.*

The time involved in Gandalaran history was huge and indistinct; I couldn't estimate how long it had been after the meteor before Zanek had become the first King. Neither could I identify when the Kingdom had gone sour or exactly when Harthim, the Last King, had bailed out from Kä and built what was now Lord City in Eddarta.

If I were analyzing this statistically, I reasoned, I'd need accurate time information and, if not actual demographics, at least some idea of the total population. Undoubtedly, the population of "Gandalarans"—that is, the favorably mutated species that would develop into this present culture—expanded exponentially at the beginning.

I reached into my Gandalaran memory, actively searching for a connection to the All-Mind's memory, but the only result was the recollection of remarks in a conversation between Ricardo—before he and Markasset had been consolidated into Rikardon—and Markasset's father, Thanasset. The older man had mentioned the Great Pleth, something Ricardo had understood as a large body of water, a lake or sea. It had been present in Gandalara when the All-Mind had achieved consciousness—that is, when the radiation-loaded meteor had struck the Great Wall above Raithskar and initiated the mutation which provided the subconscious memory link. Some geologic change—possibly an earthquake triggered by the impact of the meteor—had caused the Great Pleth to diminish and, as far as Thanasset or Markasset knew, disappear entirely. Centers of population had begun to shift toward the walls and the only remaining sources of water.

These impassable walls made Gandalara a closed world, I thought, and let the vision form of the humanoid race, little more than animals, growing in numbers, developing social structure, establishing territories. Foraging for edible plants shifted into planting and cultivating them; a circle of shelters became a town; surplus food appeared, allowing leisure time for the development of tools which would help insure a greater surplus, and more time to spend inventing and creating.

They would have been living between the edge of the sea and the edge of their world, the walls, I thought. *There would have been a long period in which the population growth filled in the new land left by the diminishing sea. But it would have been only a matter of time before the retreating shoreline exposed only untenable land. The pressure of continued population growth would have initiated a period of intense competition for tenable land area.*

War.

I sighed.

Unpalatable as the idea is, war is an effective deterrent to population growth. Trouble is, it becomes a habit.

Zanek must have had the vision to see what was happening. With the Great Pleth shrinking and already huge desert areas growing, the environment was threatening everybody, and cooperation was the only road to survival.

Markasset, of course, had a built-in reverence for the legendary First King. But Ricardo, too, appreciated what I knew of the man. He had enforced peace, promoted trade, and used the telepathic power of the Ra'ira in some benevolent way to help him. The Bronze—the thin sheet of imprinted metal which concealed the vault door in the Council Chamber, and which Tarani had been able to decipher—had cautioned future Kings in their use of the Ra'ira.

"Seek out the discontented"; it had commanded, "Give them answer, not penalty."

Zanek was a wise man, I thought. *No wonder he and the Kings who followed his way were so loved.*

But the other Kings—only half of the present world believe that they had any good points.

I almost laughed. *Half of the world,* I repeated to myself. *I think I've found the answer. The All-Mind isn't geographically limited to one half of the world or the other, but people are. For instance, look at Thanasset. He's as strongly linked to the All-Mind as anyone who isn't a Recorder. But his knowledge and opinions are hardly universal.*

He told me that the Ra'ira had been delivered into the hands of the Kings after Kä had begun to demand slaves.

Wrong. Zanek had it at the beginning.

He spoke of the Great Pleth as if there had been only one sea.

Wrong. The Chizan crossings mark a division of Gandalara, and the composition of the desert on this side bears every earmark of once having been covered by a salt sea, just like the Kapiral on Raithskar's side.

And he believes that Serkajon's sword was the only steel sword that had ever existed in Gandalara.

Which Zefra swears is wrong.

I stopped the whirling chain of logic and took a mental breather, and approached the conclusion calmly.

In high school, Ricardo had a world history textbook that looked nearly new except for one short, dog-eared section on Greek and Roman mythology—a testament that students study most conscientiously the subjects which are most interesting to them. Perhaps the All-Mind knows everything about the history of this world, but people look only at that part of it which favors their ethical system. If enough individuals unconsciously draw selectively on their links to the All-Mind, part of past history becomes a current belief system. To Raithskarians, Serkajon is a hero. To Eddartans—the Lords, at least—he is a thief and a traitor.

All of which adds up to—don't believe everything you hear.

Has Raithskar mistakenly forgotten about a second sword, or has Eddarta mistakenly remembered it?

15

I snapped into the present, anxiety closing my throat so that I could hardly breathe. We were leaving behind the Ra'ira and Serkajon's sword—*my* sword—to go look for a centuries-lost treasure which might or might not exist. Suddenly all the doubts I had felt when Zefra and Tarani had talked about this project swept down on me—only now something was missing, a layer of dullness, a barrier of simply not caring. Now I was fully awake, fully alert...

And I haven't been, I realized. *Between the time Keeshah left us* (one thing hadn't changed; pain still zinged through me when I thought of the big cat) *and that—um, what happened in the cellar—I wasn't really here for the full count. But now my head is clear; my mind is functioning again. Well enough to realize we may be doing exactly the wrong thing.*

"How do you know there's another sword?" I asked.

Tarani jumped, and we stopped walking. We had left behind the last buildings of the city, and we had outdistanced most of the other travelers. At the moment, there was no one nearby.

"How do I know?" Tarani repeated. "It seems logical to me. The Captain of the Sharith would not have so valuable an article if it were unique."

"A King who wanted to cement the loyalty of the Sharith might give a unique weapon to the Captain," I argued.

"Not even Zanek would have done that," she said, shaking her head. "Rakor was even more rare and valuable then than now. The only reason to give up so rich a gift would be for the very purpose Eddarta's legends report—the symbology of twin swords, shared between King and Captain."

"Do you *know* that, Tarani?" I asked.

"I do not understand what you mean," Tarani said, but shifted her weight restlessly.

"Zefra said you have a strong link with the All-Mind," I

108

said. "Is that how you know? Have you seen it in the All-Mind?"

Tarani shook her head, not in answer, but at me. "You have strange notions, Rikardon. One does not 'see' in that sense without establishing a direct link."

"You mean, like through a Recorder?"

"Yes," she said, and turned abruptly. Before she could walk away, I caught her arm. She froze, and I moved my hand away quickly.

"You went to Recorder's school, Tarani. Can you—"

"*No!*" She didn't move, didn't look at me. "I did not complete the study. I am not a Recorder."

"All I want," I said, still speaking to the side of her face, "is more assurance that we're going *to* something, instead of *from* something. We're leaving the Ra'ira in Indomel's control, and that bothers me, Tarani. Isn't there some way you can—"

"You accepted the plan in Lord City," Tarani interrupted. "Why do you question it now?"

"I—we—that is, I seem to be able to think more clearly. Now."

I steeled myself to tell her, if she asked, that the shock of pleasure she had given me in Carn's cellar had offset the shock of Keeshah's loss. But she didn't ask. She looked at me for an instant, then lowered her eyes and nodded.

"That," she said softly, "I understand very well."

Well, I'll be—I thought. *Her, too? Maybe it wasn't just Keeshah's going that left me in that fog. It might have been the whole trauma of being captured, when we were so close to escape. With everything else involved, it might have been nothing more than the ordinary distraction of wanting each other and denying ourselves. That makes the most sense, considering that relief came when desire was satisfied.*

Tarani glanced over her shoulder. We were still far ahead of any others, but we could hear them behind us, see them dimly in the wavering lamplight.

"There is no time to debate it now, Rikardon. We are committed to leaving Eddarta."

"Not until we meet our contacts," I said. "We could slip back and..."

"And be killed trying to steal the Ra'ira?" she demanded.

"And kill Obilin and get Rika back," I answered. "You need a sword; that's a sword."

109

" 'Kill Obilin' is hardly so simple a task," she said. "And you must know, as well as I, that Indomel will not spare us if we are recaptured. Please, Rikardon, it is my *judgment* that the other sword truly exists, and that we shall be able to find it. Let us leave Eddarta now, while we are so close to freedom."

"We'll find it easily, no doubt," I said, "with the help of *my* ancestral link to the other sword?"

Tarani waved her hand dismissively. "That was pure invention, to convince Zefra of your importance in the plan," she said. "She does have power, and she believes strongly in my right—my *sole* right—to rule Eddarta."

I couldn't help feeling some resentment as I remembered the scene, but I was glad to note that the anger didn't return, as well. *Good to put things in perspective again*, I thought.

"That's why you put the compulsion on me," I said. "So that I wouldn't act surprised and put the lie to your story."

We were silent for a moment, then Tarani said: "I think I see, now, the reason for your anger. It was not that I compelled you, but that my compulsion showed distrust. Is it not so?"

"It is exactly so," I admitted.

"Even as yours," she said, "my mind was clouded then. But as we have walked, I have thought it through once more. Rika, even should we be able to reclaim it, is still a symbol of betrayal to the Lords. It is the other sword we need to defeat Indomel. Please, Rikardon, show me the trust you would have asked of me earlier."

She stopped talking and I hesitated before answering. I wanted to trust her. I didn't want to hurt her. But I also wanted to *know* we were doing the right thing. Once we were all the way out of Eddarta, it might be harder to get back safely than it had been to leave—which, so far, I wouldn't have called a picnic.

"I am not a Recorder," she repeated, when she sensed the way I was leaning. Her voice had an edge—of impatience, of fear, of something I didn't understand. "What you would ask of me is beyond my skill." She whirled abruptly and took two steps down the road, stopped and looked back. She held out her hand.

"Are we not together, Rikardon?" she asked softly.

I took her hand and squeezed it, unable to say anything around the fear that had lodged in my throat at the very hint that we might be separated again. I released her fingers, to

110

let her draw her hand away if she wished—but it pressed warmly into mine as we started south again.

Markasset didn't know much about Recorder training, I thought, *but then I don't expect anybody besides Recorders know much about it. Tarani mentioned, though, that she had gone into school younger than most students—and Zefra told us that she had asked Volitar to be alert for signs of the mindgift in her daughter. So how young was young? Was she six? Seven? And she left at fifteen. Time enough, surely, to have had a lot of practice at whatever they do. Surely, she couldn't have forgotten her training.*

So there must be another reason why she won't try for a link. Maybe there is a special piece of training that constitutes graduation from Recorder's school, that Tarani missed. Maybe it's just that she feels guilty about not finishing.

Now there's another thought. She probably doesn't really know why she left, what with Antonia just dropping in on her like that—

Antonia...

A memory came to me clearly from the cellar.

She called me Ricardo, I remembered, astonishment freezing me for a moment, so that my pace slowed.

"What is wrong?" Tarani asked me.

"Nothing," I said, falling into step with her again and thinking: *She called me Rikardon, too.* I grinned foolishly at Tarani, the only expression I would allow myself of the joy that shouted and sang all along my nerve ends. "I—it's just—I'm *glad* we're together."

All four of us, I added, feeling a little crazy. *Ricardo, Markasset, Tarani, and Antonia.*

Tarani glanced sideways at me, obviously still puzzled, but she seemed willing to let it drop. "I, too, am glad," she said.

Or are there five of us? I wondered, feeling a little giddy. *Rikardon seems to be a newcomer, a little different from both Ricardo and Markasset. When Antonia and Tarani blend, there may even be six of us. Think of it, six . . .*

When they blend?

What if they don't? Markasset was dead, after all, and Ricardo needed only to absorb his memories, not his personality. It may not be possible for the same thing to happen for Tarani and Antonia.

Yet I didn't awaken in Gandalara as Rikardon. Markasset

*and Ricardo were separate until Thanasset gave me Rika.
When I touched that steel sword . . .*

Holy great day in the morning!

I felt a chill crawling up my arms, lifting the hairs and
raising bumps on my skin. It was no more comfortable for
being familiar by now. It was fear and eagerness, denial and
commitment, bewilderment and comprehension.

It was a sense of destiny. _

*There is another Gandalaran body with two personalities.
And there is another steel sword.*

There is another sword, I admitted. *But we're not going
after it to make Tarani the High Lord of Eddarta. We're
looking for it to make Tarani whole.*

Since my arrival in Gandalara, I had been struggling with
my "destiny". At first I had let myself believe that I needed
only to clear Markasset's father of complicity in the theft of
the jewel. It was only in Dyskornis, where I had discovered
the Ra'ira's special powers and the defense my dualness
provided, that I had accepted what seemed to be my true
charge—to return the care of the Ra'ira to the hands of
honorable men.

I wasn't really unhappy with that decision. Ricardo had
spent a pleasant, productive life with the feeling that in
teaching languages he was performing a service of importance
to society. Markasset had felt no sense of purpose, and had
drifted uneasily through his short life.

I couldn't help feeling a little grateful, too. I had been
given a young body, a chance at a second life, a friendship
bond with Keeshah that had been sustaining and delightful.
It seemed that one task in return for that was not too high a
price for what I had gained, especially when I was uniquely
equipped to perform that task.

I felt exasperated and not a little scared, however, by the
piecemeal way "destiny" was revealing itself to me, and by
the many opportunities for choice. It would have been easier
if I had believed that I was the agent for a conscious,
thinking, supernatural force, and that I could count on protection and a sense of commitment from such a being. But
that image didn't jibe with reality, with the way I had
stumbled into and through things, with all the chances I had
had to go in the wrong direction.

And if this isn't proof that there's nobody home, I thought,
I don't know what would be. Even a kindergarten-level god

should have been able to foresee the need for that fool sword. Why couldn't we have brought it with us, instead of traipsing clear back across the world to get it now? I wondered, then sighed.

No use pretending this development bothers me, I admitted. *The truth is, I'm in full agreement with this particular step along our twisting path—though I'd rather we were riding Keeshah.* (The familiar, painful twinge of loss.) *Whatever happens when Tarani touches that other sword, it should at least give Tarani some answers to the confusion she must have been feeling.*

So for once, "destiny", I shouted mentally, *I'm on your side. For my own reasons, it's true. I love Tarani and Antonia, and I think they're both fond of me. I want them to be at peace with one another, work together.* Then *we'll talk about who's going to be high mucky-muck in Eddarta.*

I lengthened my stride. Tarani matched it, a look of relief flashing across her face as she sensed that, for whatever reasons, I was now fully committed to finding the second steel sword before we returned to Eddarta.

"We're almost there," I said, pointing ahead.

The lines of lamps on either side of our avenue merged with four others that had followed the other two main roads from the city. Beyond the edge of the bright pool of light at their merging point was a ridge of darkness, and above it the pale clouds. The ridge was a virtual wall of the reeds that grew along the edge of the rivers. The roads from the city emptied here into a main east-west thoroughfare that wound along a western branch of the Tashal, one side of the road always bordered by reeds. In the farming areas, the reeds were sometimes trimmed down.

The Lords would have designated reed harvesters, of course, who were authorized to sell the reeds to weavers, furniture makers, paper mills, mine suppliers. But there were also some areas where the reeds were an obstruction to the short-distance water transport system. And I suspected that farmers, by nature and necessity more independent than their city-dwelling counterparts, didn't waste the reeds they removed to give walking room to the vleks which pulled the rafts.

Here the reeds grew in their natural state, thickly clustered, man-high, their delicate fern-like top growth waving

113

slightly as the sluggish bank water stirred the bases of the reeds.

Short of the dark barrier, however, was a bright circle of light—entirely empty.

"Why is no one there?" Tarani asked uneasily.

"I doubt they'll show themselves before we arrive," I answered.

That's logical, I thought, as we stepped into the circle of light and looked around, waiting for the people who were to meet us to appear. *So why am I worried?*

I could not help feeling exposed here. There was something eerie about the empty, lighted area, so quiet, waiting...

"It's too quiet," I said.

There were Gandalaran counterparts to most of the life forms Ricardo had known, including the noisy varieties of insects and amphibians who lived in and near water. The river bank was silent, except for the rustling of reeds as they moved to the current's pressure.

"Why would it be this quiet?" I asked

We heard noise then—behind us. Vleks. Upset. Men. Shouting.

"What could that be?" Tarani asked as we looked back toward the ruckus. There was a small rise between us and the travelers who had fallen behind us; we couldn't see what was going on.

"Vleks aren't fond of dralda," said a voice from behind us, sinister, amused.

"Oh no," I said, turning slowly, releasing Tarani's hand and stepping a bit away from her. "Obilin, how in the name of Zanek did you find us?"

The small man had stepped out from the reeds. Now two dralda melted into the edge of the lamplight, much closer to us than Obilin was. Silent until now, they growled softly and the fur behind their heads seemed to tremble with anticipation.

Tarani took a breath and tensed—and Obilin nodded to someone behind me. Before I could react, an arm whipped around my throat, and the bronze blade of a thin dagger gleamed in front of my face. I gripped the arm with my hands and pulled at it, gasping for breath.

"Do let him breathe, Sharam," Obilin said, and the tension in the muscular arm eased slightly.

"You can't control both the man and the dralda," Obilin said to Tarani. "And they all have orders to kill your friend if anything, um, unusual happens. Do you understand me?"

Tarani nodded.

Here we are again, I thought bitterly. *Tarani bound because of me.* There was no despair this time, however, only fury—and a determination to find a way out of the trap. Amid the frantic creation and rejection of plans was a small kernel of pleasure in being *able* to "think on my feet" again.

Obilin laughed. "To answer your question, Rikardon, I didn't need to *find* you, only *wait* for you. I knew as soon as the messages from Lingis stopped that you were behind it, and that you were free. You had to be coming to Eddarta. When Zefra convinced that fool Indomel that the lady Tarani was too ill to meet with him, I knew the two of you were together and on your way out of the city. I and Sharam and the dralda have been waiting here for you since noon." He shook his foot, spraying water on the nearer dralda, which jumped, snarled, and edged away. "Uncomfortably, I might add, and at the cost of an excellent pair of boots."

Since noon, I thought. *What happened to our contacts? Has he scared them away?* Then something else Obilin had said penetrated.

"Indomel doesn't know Tarani's gone?" I asked.

"No. Nor you, either, for that matter. The High Lord has been preoccupied lately. The silence from Lingis disturbed him, of course, but I persuaded him to wait for more definite information before he took any rash action."

"You mean against me," Tarani said. "Indomel would have killed me if he had been certain Rikardon had escaped. You protected us both. Why?"

"That's easy to figure," I answered, before Obilin could speak. "He wants you for himself, Tarani, and he needs *me* to control *you*. When Indomel finally figures out we're gone, he'll pretend to look for us, and fail. The High Lord won't be happy with him, but Obilin will have plenty of compensation for that—you and me, hidden away and in his power."

Obilin smiled grimly. "Well stated," he said. "And entirely accurate. Our—shall we call it our trysting place, my dear?" He bowed mockingly to Tarani. She merely glared at him, and he laughed. "In any case, it is prepared for us, and it's time we were on our way. The trip will be more comfortable for all of us if you both cooperate. We shall not, obviously, be traveling by the road. The dralda over there—" He nodded to the roadway behind us, from which there still came the sounds of mass confusion "—are keeping potential witnesses

115

at a distance. They will be allowed to pass, once we are safely off the roadway. Shall we go, please? *Now.*"

Obilin gestured to us with his sword, and the man behind me started dragging me off to my left. I went with him, staggering but not struggling. I was watching Tarani as Obilin approached her. There was a look about her, one I had seen when she walked on stage and prepared to dance—

Tarani burst into flame just before Obilin's hand touched her. He jerked his hand back in surprise, but with startling quickness recovered and reached out again. "From now on, your skill will serve me instead of trick me," he promised grimly, grabbing a tongue of flame that shimmered back into the shape of Tarani's arm. "Sharam, cut the lady's friend. Just a little."

"No!" Tarani shouted, and lunged in my direction. Obilin's grip held her back, but Sharam's attention had been distracted just enough.

I grabbed the hand that held the dagger with both my hands, braced my feet on the ground, and arched my body, pushing his arm over my head. The movement threw Sharam off balance; he staggered backward, grunting and straining to bring his arm down again.

"Mara," Sharam grunted, and the dralda on my side of the lighted circle launched itself at me. Obviously following orders from its master, it turned at the last minute and broadsided into me, knocking the wind from my lungs and tumbling me and Sharam off the edge of the road into the spongy ground cover.

The double shock of the dralda hitting me and my slamming full-length into Sharam as we fell made my head swim and loosened my grip. Sharam had taken a knock, too. He pulled his knife hand free, but in the process loosened his hold around my neck. I rolled to the left, striking back with my elbow.

We were nearly out of range of the light. I felt, rather than saw, the knife swing by me, a miss too near to bear thinking about. Both dralda were at the edge of the road, ready to lunge. I pulled out my sword, bracing for the attack.

"Stop!" Tarani called, and the dogs pulled back, shaking their heads furiously, whining.

"Tass, Mara, attack!" Sharam said, no longer interested in Obilin's need to keep me alive. He moved into the light, swung his arm at me. "Attack!"

116

Obilin's sword pressed into Tarani's side. "Release them," he ordered. They came at me.

The first beast ran right onto the point of my sword. I rolled back and used its body as a shield. The other dralda concentrated on my unprotected legs and I kicked out and scrabbled around, trying to keep free of its teeth and claws. The weight of the dead one made breathing difficult, and its fur muffled and garbled the noises around me.

I recognized the howling I remembered from the desert—it came from the direction of Eddarta, and frighteningly close. And I heard voices. Their tone was angry or fearful, but only a few words reached me clearly.

"Sharam, I told you to leave the others—" Obilin's voice.

"I *did*; I *am* telling them; they aren't—" Sharam.

Obilin's voice again, menacing. "It is *your* doing."

The sound of bronze striking bronze, then Tarani's voice.

"Too slow, Obilin. You fleason," she spat at him, and, had I not been quite so busy, I would have shuddered at the contempt and power in her voice. As it was, I found myself listening more carefully.

"I would kill him with my own hands, and then destroy myself, before I would allow you to command me as Molik did!"

The howling came closer, stopped abruptly.

"There," I heard Obilin say. "You may have the mindgift, whore, but Sharam knows his animals. They are *his*, not *yours*."

"Are they?" Tarani's voice said, then: "*Attack*."

The second dralda stopped worrying me; I pushed the dead one away, relieved beyond words to be free of its musky smell, and watched three dralda stalk Obilin and Sharam as Tarani, sword and dagger both ready in her hands, backed through the line of animals toward me. The big, wild-looking dogs were silent except for skin-tensing growls.

"No," Sharam shouted, pointing at me with one hand, Tarani with the other. "*They* are the prey. Attack!"

The dralda stopped, looked back at us, hesitating.

"Attack, I said!" Sharam yelled, and grabbed the nearest one by the fur at its shoulders. He lifted, pulled, tried to turn the animal, then howled in pain as powerful jaws closed on his wrist.

That seemed to decide things. I caught a glimpse of Obilin

backing away from a lunging dralda—but I was moving, myself, by then.

Tarani was right behind me; we ran west along the road. I was trying not to listen to the noise behind us—yelling, snapping, chewing.

Or the sound beside me—sobbing.

A shape loomed up in the dimness of the road; Tarani and I skidded to a halt and crouched back, ready for another fight.

"No!" a scared voice cried, while the shape backed away hastily, hands upraised. "I came to meet you. Carn? Tellor's caravan?"

"You were supposed to be at the joining," I said.

"You didn't find enough people already there?" the voice asked sarcastically. "You're lucky I stuck around when I saw who else was waiting for you."

True, I thought.

"All right," I said. "Now what?"

The faceless man dragged us into the reeds, where a small, damp clearing had been cut away. Another man waited for us there, and the two of them exchanged clothes with us.

"The usual plan," the first man said, "is for us to step back out on the road and pretend we're you. I think we'll change that plan, considering."

"You'll have to hurry," the other man said. "There's a river crossing about an hour west of here. Take it, and go straight north—no roads, mind you, *directly* north.

"That's the only way you can hope to find Tellor's caravan by dawn. He knows you're coming, but he won't wait for you." They slapped us on the back, and pushed us out toward the road.

"Good fortune," followed us as a whisper.

16

It was nearly dawn before Tarani and I spoke again. We had located Tellor's caravan and were watching the bustle of camp-breaking.

"Do your clothes fit well?" I asked

"They fit," she said. "They smell *vile*."

I had already noticed that.

"Vleks," I said. "I don't think we can look forward to a fun trip."

"I prefer the company of vleks," she said drily, "to that of Lords or dralda."

"Thank you, Tarani," I said, and she looked at me.

In the growing light, I could see the lines at eyecorners and around her mouth—they seemed to be a fixture now, worn in by the strain of the past few weeks. I wanted to smooth these lines with my fingertips, but I held back.

Time, I reminded myself. *Give her time*.

"Why do you thank me?" Tarani asked.

"Your work with the dralda saved us," I said. We both knew that wasn't what I really meant, so I stumbled on. "Thank you for what you said to Obilin."

She drew into herself, holding her shoulders, and turned her face away. "What I did to the dralda—it destroyed them," she said in a small voice. "And as for what I said to Obilin, I spoke in anger—"

She stopped, caught her breath, started again.

"That is untrue," she said. "I meant what I said. Molik was—was *filthy* inside. Thymas was sweet and kind and joyful—but he felt desire only, and that for—not for me, but for the image I allowed him to see. Being with him was more pleasant, and did not involve my gift, but it was not—not basically different from what I had done for Molik."

She snapped around to face me, her dark eyes shining in a way I had never seen before but I would never forget.

"At last I have been touched with love, Rikardon. I shall not permit any other kind of touch."

I leaned toward her, wanting more than anything to hold her against me, just to hold her. But she stepped back and laughed shakily, deliberately lifting the intense mood.

"And in that line of thought," she said, "perhaps it would be best if those on the caravan believe me to be a man."

I forced myself to think instead of want, and I considered her suggestion.

"We'll be on the road for a long time," I said. "A sustained illusion would drain your strength, and we may need it later."

She jumped at that. "You mean Obilin—surely not!"

"No," I said, praying that I was right. "I mean Worfit."

"The roguelord from Raithskar," she said, nodding. "We will need to pass through Chizan, which he controls now."

"And your skill will help us there," I added. "So—" I looked closely at the people moving in the melee of bawling vleks. "It seems there *are* female vlek handlers," I said. I smiled at her. "But do wear your scarf," I cautioned her. "There must be fewer dark-headed handlers than female handlers."

"As you say." She pulled a soiled and wrinkled scarf from her belt, made a face when she sniffed at it, then arranged it over the short, silky fur to hide it. Then she adjusted her weapons—nobody traveled the desert in Gandalara unarmed, so they weren't out of place—and threw back her shoulders. "I am ready," she said.

We went down to meet Tellor, who turned out to be a large man, beefy with muscles, with a rough and physical sense of humor. A joke was met with a roaring laugh and a backslap that, often as not, sent you face-first into the sand. After acknowledging our arrival, appraising Tarani's body with inoffensive appreciation, and turning us over to the vlekmaster, he never spoke to us.

Tellor mastered the caravan. That is, he had contracted with a number of merchants to move them and their goods across the desert. This particular caravan was made up of only very rich merchants, who brought not only goods for sale, but retinues of servants and "sales help"—men and women who would sit within a circle of goods at the markets and talk price to prospective buyers. There were also mercenary guards and us—the vlek handlers.

The vleks were goat-size, with spindly legs, dull minds,

and unpleasant dispositions. They were the means for moving trade goods, the poles and distinctly colored awnings that marked a merchant's market territory, food and water for the whole caravan, sleeping pallets, feed for themselves, and personal travel supplies for Tellor, the merchants, and their people.

A vlek couldn't carry more than about a hundred pounds of stuff on its back, but two to four of the creatures could be harnessed to deep-bedded, two-wheeled carts and the load in the cart could be, perhaps, a third heavier than the total weight manageable by the vleks individually.

If I had had the time to think about it, I would have expected the caravan to be heading for Iribos, the closest Refreshment House to Eddarta. Since Carn had mentioned Vasklar and Stomestad specifically, I would have assumed that the Fa'aldu slave route led from Iribos north and east to the big Refreshment House at which we had left a wounded Thymas on our first approach to Eddarta.

I would have been wrong, so I was just as glad I'd never thought about it. Tellor's caravan was bound on the northern route, aimed directly for Stomestad. A map would have shown it as ten man-days from Eddarta, and normal caravan travel (vlek-speed) would have stretched the time to the two seven-days Carn had mentioned. But this caravan was so big that there were more carts than usual and a lower vlek/cart proportion, so that the animals tired quickly and the wide-based wheels of the carts slowed us down.

It took us twenty-two miserable days to reach the Refreshment House at Stomestad.

In all that time, Tarani and I had little time for speech, none at all for privacy. For the first few days, the work was borderline interesting, as learning any new job can be. But once it became "routine"—that is, as soon as we could perform all the required tasks with dependable competence— it became only work—nasty, hard work.

I had hoped that familiarity with vleks would give me an appreciation of some positive quality I hadn't yet seen in the animals.

Not a chance.

Vleks bawled and bucked and did their best to bite the handler when they were harnessed, loaded, unharnessed, unloaded, fed, or penned in the ridiculous pole-and-rope enclosure that was thrown up every night. They never seemed to be quiet. At night—well, there were over a hundred of them crowded in together, nearly half of them female. For vleks, the odds were that at least five females would be in season at any one time.

We didn't get much rest.

The trip wasn't made more pleasant by the two-legged company, either. Vlek handlers are—to put it kindly—a lower-class crowd. Had I been alone, I might have enjoyed their rough humor and foul language. That, in itself, didn't bother Tarani; she had traveled with caravans before, though not in just this way. What bothered us both was that most of the women who became vlek handlers were the type who didn't object to being the prize in the nightly mondea game.

We were informed of this tradition on the first night.

Tarani objected.

So did I.

It took five nights of her refusal and my bruises to convince the other handlers that we were atypical—and, at that, we were never quite sure they *were* convinced. So we stayed close together at night, and only one of us slept at a time.

The snatches of rest, brief as they were, brought me pleasant but unremembered dreams that always left me feeling better —calm and almost happy, at least until the needs of our situation made themselves felt. Tarani, too, seemed to waken twice at each rising: once from sleep, and again from an open-eyed daze. But Tarani's face revealed a fleeting expression of *fear* before she moved on about the day's business.

I asked her about it once.

"It is nothing, really," she said. "I have dreams which are . . . odd. Fatigue and tension, doubtless, are causing them."

She didn't invite further discussion, and I didn't press the issue. I didn't want to discuss her dreams either, because I thought I knew what they were.

It was obvious these weren't the ordinary sort of nightmares— waking from those would have produced relief at the realization they were only dreams. It seemed to me the dreams, in themselves, were not the problem. Rather, Tarani was disturbed by the fact that she was having that particular kind of dream—she had said "dreams", so it wasn't one dream, repeating itself.

I'll bet it's Antonia, I thought to myself. *Trying to assert control? Or just remembering? I should think that, for a*

Gandalaran, dreaming about a world two-thirds covered with water would be a distressingly alien experience.

Like me, Tarani quickly shed the after-effect of her dreams, and we were both kept too busy to think about it much.

We reached Stomestad at last. Tellor called out the ritual request for shelter; the symbolic cloth gates were opened; the vleks were led in.

Stomestad was the largest of all the Refreshment Houses, but by the time Tellor, the merchants, and all their people had settled into the four-bed cubicles that lined one long wall of the courtyard, there were few sheltered beds left. Those were assigned by lottery to the rest of us; since the caravan would stay in Stomestad for several days, chances were, nearly all of us would get at least one night's sleep indoors.

Neither Tarani nor I won the first lottery. I was disappointed, but when I looked around to commiserate with Tarani, I couldn't find her anywhere in the crowd gathered outside the Refreshment House entrance. I panicked (wondering who *else* was missing) until I caught a flash of movement at the edge of my vision. A familiar white shape was just sinking out of my line of sight, around the corner of the rectangular, walled enclosure of Stomestad.

A hand tugged at my sleeve. I looked down to see a small boy, dressed in a child-size version of the long white tunic that the Fa'aldu always wore in their dealings with travelers.

"Sir," the boy began nervously. I smiled; he grinned back at me and went on with more confidence. "If it please you, sir, the Respected Elder invites you and the lady to speak with him privately."

I remembered the boy from our earlier visit—he was a nephew of Vasklar, the "Respected Elder" in question.

"Thank you, Hil," I said, and the boy beamed at the sound of his name. "We will come quickly."

The boy ran through the opening in the salt-block wall that was the only entrance to the compound. I ignored the curious stares of the crew, who had been too far away to hear what the boy had said, and headed around the corner.

Tarani was playing with Lonna—catching her in the circle of her arms, "letting" the bird slip through and spread her wings to fly, then catching her again. When I appeared, the play stopped, and Lonna took to the air. Tarani came toward me, looking puzzled.

"Still no sign of pursuit," she said.

We had seen Lonna frequently during the trip, but caution had dictated that the bird not join us and make us even more noticeable than we were already. But Tarani had been in continuous contact with Lonna. At first the news of a clear backtrail had been good; then it had begun to worry us.

"I do not like it," Tarani said, emphatically. "Indomel must know, by now, that we are both gone. Granted that he cannot know where we are, I would expect him to search every possible route from Eddarta."

I shrugged. "He has the Ra'ira," I said, "and you proved to be little help with learning how to use it. Maybe he's just decided to cut his losses and be glad you aren't in Eddarta, stirring up trouble."

Her eyes narrowed.

"Do you believe that?" she demanded.

"No," I said, and laughed. "Listen, I've got good news and bad news."

"I beg your pardon?" she said.

At last a permanent contribution to Gandalaran culture, I thought. *A cliché joke.*

"The bad news is," I said, "that we lost the lottery."

She groaned.

"The good news is, Vasklar just sent for us."

Tarani brightened. "Then we won't be expected to maintain this—" She slapped her arm. "—fleabitten disguise any longer."

"Not if I have anything to say about it," I promised.

Lonna dropped down to hover in front of me for a moment. I stroked her breast feathers gently, careful not to pull them in the wrong direction as the thick muscles beneath them moved with the slow rhythm of her wingbeat. The bird dipped to Tarani for a similar caress, then took to the sky.

I shaded my eyes with my hand to watch her go, until her white body was indistinguishable from the cloud layer.

"Lonna remembers Keeshah," Tarani said quietly, slipping her hand into mine. "Her image of you is always blended with that of the sha'um." She paused. "Rikardon, will Keeshah return?"

We seem to know each other so well, I thought. *I forget that I have to tell her some things before she knows them.*

"When this happened to my—to Markasset's—father, his sha'um never returned from the Valley."

"But surely that is rare?" Tarani said. "Thymas talked of this once, and he said that the sha'um are gone for a year.

124

Among the Sharith, they believe the sha'um stay in the Valley long enough to see their cubs born and sheltered to a certain age. But no one knows. Those who return do not remember—or at least do not speak of—what occurred in the Valley."

"Did Thymas say that they *always* return?" I asked.

"No." Sadly, pressing my hand. "This must be very hard for you, my love."

I reached for her then. She came into my arms, but I could feel her trembling. As the seconds passed and the overwhelming need we'd shared in Carn's cellar didn't reappear, she relaxed and returned my embrace.

Too soon for me, we stepped apart and went to see Vasklar.

The Elder was truly old, his headfur dark and patchy. He was scandalized when he saw us, and he sent children scurrying to the bath-house to prepare tubs scented with dried herbs. They were small tubs, little more than big water troughs made of rough tile. Compared to the deep, ceramic-lined tub in Thanasset's home in Raithskar, they weren't much.

Compared to twenty-two days in the unwashed company of vleks and their handlers, it was paradise.

When we were clean and wearing borrowed clothes, Tarani and I joined the Stomestad family at their huge dining table in the inner courtyard. It was a privilege shared by few non-Fa'aldu; I owed it to Balgokh, the Elder at Yafnaar who had helped me and taken a liking to me. He had spread the word to the other Refreshment Houses. Among the Fa'aldu, I was a celebrity. Tarani—known to them before this as the dancer and illusionist—was welcomed on my account.

At dinner, I recounted the edited story of my arrival in Raithskar, wherein Markasset had lost his memory, mended his loose ways, and helped his father, and had been rewarded with the steel sword, recovered memories, and a new name. The Stomestad had heard it before, but they received it with as much show of pleasure as when I had first told it. I dared not look at Tarani, sure that she was gaping at me in amazement. She had heard part of the story in a different version; she thought I was a Visitor.

It's the pits, trying to remember who I've told what to, I thought. *If this sword pulls Tarani and Antonia together—wouldn't it be wonderful to be able to tell somebody the whole truth for a change?*

And what will Tarani think when she hears it? I wondered.

I've been lying to her about myself since the day I met her. I hope she won't hate me for it.

After we had eaten, Vasklar escorted Tarani and me into a private sitting room.

"And now, my friends," he said. "I will not ask what happened in Eddarta. Thymas and the two Sha'um are missing, Rika is not at your side, and you come back to us in the manner of an escape. That speaks clearly enough of disaster. So I ask only: how else may I be of service to you?"

"Vasklar, we are grateful beyond words for everything you and your people have already done for us," I said. "At this point, we need only what you would provide any traveler—time to rest, and food and water to send us on our way."

"And where does your way lead?" Vasklar asked, squinting at me in the lamplight.

"Through Chizan," I said. "Back to Raithskar."

"A long journey," Vasklar said. "From here to Chizan, what route?"

I exchanged a look with Tarani, and knew we were in agreement on this point.

"The quickest way possible," I said. "Straight across the desert."

Vasklar didn't argue with us. "The Strofaan is the worst of the deserts," he said. "And the quantity of water you would need—"

His voice trailed off as his mind turned inward, figuring. Tarani spoke into the silence. "Lonna is still with us, Vasklar," she said. "She can carry small amounts of water. If you will provide that, and feed her when she visits—"

Vasklar smiled, his eyes nearly disappearing in wrinkles. "I am old enough that I recognize change when I see it coming," he said, "but still too young to predict its nature. I do know that you two are special in the world, and the agents of change. And knowing this part of the world as I do, I must assume that change will be an improvement.

"Of course, we will provide whatever you need, my friends. Go now to your rest."

We had been given one of the family's guest rooms. Shallow, wide salt blocks created a big platform in one corner of the room, and it was covered by a rich, fluffy pallet.

A double bed, I thought. *And the usual courtesy of asking what arrangement we preferred was noticeably absent. Ei-*

ther the Stomestad Fa'aldu are getting crowded, or the way Tarani and I feel about one another is patently obvious.

We were exhausted, just out of one desert and very much aware that we were about to head into another one. Tarani and I slept together in that bed for eight nights and never touched except to kiss lightly morning and evening. There was no tension, no strain, no urgency. There was caring and togetherness and the pleasure of being secure among friends. I caught the look that told me Tarani's dreams still disturbed her, but even with that, it was a comfortable time.

On the morning we were to leave, the courtyard was deserted. Tellor's caravan had departed, unmourned and apparently quite efficient without us, two days earlier. Vasklar walked with us to the gate and, according to the ritual, returned our weapons.

"I would ask one favor of you," he said. "When you reach Chizan, send word to us that you are safe. Speak to Pornon, at the High Crossing Inn. The Inn is our last stop for the slaves we help. Take this—" He handed us a thin strip of leather that carried inked Gandalaran characters that made no sense.

Code, I thought. The High Crossing Inn must be the "safe house" Jaris mentioned, and this is the way the Fa'aldu find out a slave is safe, so they can release Jaris's commission for payment.

"Pornon will take it to a maufel who is also one of us," Vasklar said as I took what he offered. "When we receive it, we will know that you are safe, and rejoice."

Tarani was the one who brought up the logic flaw. "You will know we have reached Chizan," she said. "Does that mean, necessarily, that we are safe?"

Vasklar chuckled. "I see your point. For escaping slaves, they are truly one and the same—the High Lord's strength does not reach into Chizan."

"Where do the slaves go after Chizan?" I asked.

"We have no idea," Vasklar answered. "It is better that way, I think. They agree not to communicate with the Fa'aldu again after they have sent back their 'safe' sign."

"Then how do you know they have truly escaped?" Tarani asked.

"By knowing that they have not been recaptured," Vasklar said. "The Fa'aldu would hear if it happened. No one," he said proudly, "who has reached Pornon in Chizan has ever been recaptured. Believe me, my friends, the former slaves who have passed through the High Crossing Inn are living now in Omergol or Raithskar, living free lives and, I trust, happier ones than those they left."

I slipped the leather strip into my pouch. "We will send it back, Vasklar. Thank you for all you've done for us."

He became serious. "You are one of the few who know my feelings about Eddarta, how I detest the slave system. When I say that I see in you the beginning of a welcome change, I am sincere. I am honored to be a part of it through any aid I have been able to offer you."

There it was again—destiny. It crawled up my spine, flushed my face, and left me absolutely tongue-tied. The admiration of men like Vasklar humbled me and frightened me.

Impulsively and timidly, Tarani stepped up to the Elder and hugged him, then shouted with laughter when he hugged her back with surprising strength.

It seemed a good omen that we were sent into the desert with laughter as our farewell.

17

Vasklar hadn't been kidding about the Strofaan Desert. I figured that, by now, I could count myself a connoisseur of deserts. On a one-to-ten scale for unpleasantness, the Strofaan rated around fifteen. When Thymas, Tarani, the two sha'um, and I had crossed its edge from Sulis to Stomestad, we had *tasted* the Strofaan, no more than that. It hadn't been palatable then; as a steady diet, it was even less appealing.

As in most of Gandalara, there wasn't much wind, so a nearly invisible fog of salty dust particles hung constantly in the air. We wore our scarves face-wrapped every minute, except when Lonna dropped down to us every day.

Knowing we could count on the bird to bring us water, we had stuffed our backpacks with bread, cheese, fruit, and dried meat—every portable foodstuff Vasklar could provide. We rested while the bird was there. We allowed ourselves to drink more than would have been wise, had we been carrying our own water supply, and ate our largest meal of each day. Then we traded Lonna's full water bags for our empty ones and sent her off again. Other meals, between her visits, were eaten more or less on the run.

We had nothing to do besides cross that desert, so we did it as fast as we could. Zaddorn had taught me a special travel pattern, and Tarani and I followed it, running or walking for four hours, resting for one. The maps I had seen didn't have the direct distance from Stomestad to Inid, the Refreshment House closest to Chizan. Apparently, it was too rough a trip to consider, if you didn't have your own private flying water tank.

I had estimated ten to twelve man-days. With our faster travel pattern, and the discomfort of the trip encouragement in itself, Tarani and I made it to Inid in six days.

In spite of the hardship of the desert crossing, I was feeling good when we reached Inid. The physical pain of the surface wounds inflicted by the dralda in Eddarta—little more than an irritation, really—had faded during the trip to Stomestad, but the shivery memory of Obilin popping up out of nowhere had been a constant shadow in my mind. Crossing the desert, devoting every ounce of energy to the simple task of survival, had cleared away the mental dross of guilt and fear, and I was simply glad to be alive and with Tarani.

The crossing hadn't involved deprivation, and this long run, so soon after the trip to Eddarta from Lingis, honed my body to a fitness level I was sure even Markasset had never matched. I felt strong and clean in a way water could never clean me. It was as if the sand had scoured away the past and left me ready to face the future.

Tarani seemed to share those feelings. Even though the Inid family welcomed us—Lonna had been making her water-runs to Inid since we had passed the midpoint of the desert—we stayed only one night, enjoying the luxury of eight full hours of sleep. Tarani seemed to be untroubled by her dreams. We were grateful for a bath, clean clothes, and more provisions, but we were eager to get on with what we had to do.

The Zantro Pass wasn't an easy crossing—too high to breathe easily; *lots* of wind and rock and dust—but we didn't have much trouble. Lonna, no longer carrying her waterbags, rode inside Tarani's tunic. The bird had worked harder than either one of us during the desert crossing, and she showed it in thinness and shortness of breath. She deserved a little cuddling, and I didn't begrudge Tarani's solicitousness toward Lonna.

But their closeness, as always, reminded me of an uncrossable distance.

I could be happy right now, I thought, *if Keeshah were with us, or even if I could talk to him. It still feels like an essential part of me is numb and useless*.

We reached the slope that overlooked Chizan at nightfall. The lights and the smell of the city were equally noticeable.

"Can we not go past?" Tarani asked.

"You remember what the Zantil was like," I said. "We'll need rest, and a fresh supply of water, before we tackle the higher crossing. And we did promise Vasklar to send word back through Pornor.

"Don't worry," I said, putting an arm around her shoulders. "Rika isn't here to identify me, and your headfur doesn't show through the scarf. With our faces wrapped—" I sniffed the air. "—which is a survival tactic in Chizan, so no one will wonder about it—we're indistinguishable from any of a hundred other travelers."

130

Tarani sighed and nodded agreement. She pulled her water pouch from her belt, poured a little water into her cupped hand, and let Lonna dip some out. She drank some and splashed the rest on her face. The bird flew off to hunt as Tarani and I walked down into Chizan.

The city hadn't changed noticeably from the time when Molik was running things. Water was still outrageously expensive; we bought some with the money Zefra had given to Tarani in Lord City which had been, through the generosity of our Fa'aldu friends, totally useless until now. I had retained my gold-filled belt through all the clothing changes, but those coins were too dangerous to spend here.

In Raithskar, though, I thought, *they won't be as noticeable. They're a fair fortune, enough to build a house ... one with room for several kids and at least one sha'um.*

Domestic bliss. I wonder if that's *anywhere in my "destiny"?*

The High Crossing Inn was easy to find—it was a three-story building made of mud-brick and stone located close to the eastern edge of the city. Like all other such establishments, it had a vlek pen for a back yard.

We'll sleep with the windows closed, I promised myself. Remembering the flea-infested pallets we'd found in Chizan on our last visit, I added: *and on the bare floor.*

We went in the front door, past an opening on our left that led to the inevitable bar/dining room. A rickety table rested at the foot of the stairs across the smallish lobby, with a man seated behind it, draped over it, and snoring loudly.

"On second thought," I whispered to Tarani, "we've got our water. Why don't we move on tonight, and sleep just this side of the pass? We can cross early in the morning." A daylight crossing of the Zantril had been bad enough; I had no desire to try it at night.

Tarani smiled. "I wonder that the plan did not occur to me," she said. "But since we have come this far, let us at least deliver the message to Pornor."

It did seem that we owed it to Vasklar. I walked over to the man asleep on the desk and poked his shoulder. He came awake quickly, and I stepped back from the dagger that appeared in his hand.

"We don't want trouble, friend," I assured him. "We're looking for Pornor."

He put away the dagger. "You found him. Sorry about pulling the knife; guess I knew falling asleep out here was risky." He stretched and yawned, displaying broad shoulders. He was younger than I had first thought, and in good shape.

I took another step backward, and dug in my pouch for the leather strip.

"Vasklar sent this—" I began, holding it out to him.

He had taken it from me before I finished, and was holding it close to the lamp, reading it. When he looked up, he was smiling.

"I've been expecting you," he said loudly. "Rooms and meals are on the house."

"We won't be staying," I said, edging Tarani toward the door. She was going willingly. Something felt funny; she sensed it too. "Just send the message to Vasklar."

I heard a brutal sound, and Tarani's arm slipped out of my hand. When I looked around, she was on the floor, unconscious. A small man, thin and wiry, stood behind her.

Except for his size and the fact that he was holding Rika, I doubt if I would have recognized Obilin.

His face and neck were crisscrossed with healed scars; he wore a patch over his left eye. When he spoke, his voice grated out in a vicious whisper.

"This is what you left me to," he said, making it clear that he was shouting inside. "But even dralda couldn't kill me. Not *me*."

The shock of seeing him was beginning to take hold, and I fought it off. *He hit Tarani*, I reminded myself, and let the anger burn away any sympathy for the mangled man. *And he'll do worse, if I let him*.

"Sharam, of course, is dead," Obilin continued. "Indomel finally figured out that you and the girl had escaped together; when the High Guard came looking for you, they found me. They took me to the High Lord, who accused me—much too late, of course—of having deliberately misled him."

The ravaged man stepped over Tarani's inert body and came slowly toward me. I backed away, trying to assess what I saw. There were a lot of scars, but they looked to be shallow, and cleanly healed. *His face might look like a sandflea track*, I thought, *but he seems to move easily enough. A slight limp on the right—not enough to slow him down much. His hands—scarred, too, maybe some loss of strength in the fingers? But Obilin never counted much on strength. It was his agility and quickness that made him a fighter to be reckoned with*.

I don't think that's changed much.

132

How the hell did he know about this place? How did he get here so fast? In the name of conscience, what does it take to kill this man?

Obilin swaggered, the familiar movement confirming his identity, complete with the danger factor.

"You'll be happy to know, Rikardon, that I confessed everything to the High Lord. Who you are. Who she was, and is. The illusionist. The whore. Indomel might have killed me, just for knowing how powerful she is. But I had a strong bargaining point.

"I knew where you were going. *Exactly* where you were going."

I backed further, glancing over my shoulder to see how much more room there was before I hit the wall beside the stairway. Behind Obilin, a small crowd had clustered in the doorway to the bar. They were watching, fascinated, not even betting on the outcome of the imminent fight.

"Of course, I had to admit to Indomel that I'd been stealing useless slaves and selling them for a profit," he said. "In order to explain that I had *also* been selling the ones who thought they were escaping safely with the aid of the Fa'aldu. They *all* come here, you see. On my last visit to Eddarta— the one during which the lady's talent captured my fascination— Pornor approached me about the scarcity of *his* trade, and we struck a deal. At that time, Jaris was the only Fa'aldu agent in the mines. Now, thanks to my encouragement, there is one in every single mine.

"They send slaves here through the Fa'aldu system. Pornor sends back their silly coded messages, and the mine agent is paid. Meanwhile, Pornor acts as *my* agent and turns them over to Molik—Worfit, now—who, um, uses them in any way he sees fit."

I thought of Yoman and Rassa, the two escaping Eddartans whose places we had taken. They had thought themselves safe, following the Fa'aldu instructions. I thought of Vasklar, of the people he thought he had saved.

"And what happens if Worfit doesn't want them?" I demanded, letting the rage grow in me, waiting for the right time to move.

"He kills them," Obilin answered with a shrug. "But he pays well for the ones he takes, and Pornor and I split the fee. It is a profitable venture."

Why is he letting me keep him talking? I wondered, suddenly suspicious.

Too late, I saw the men on the stairway. They lunged at me, grabbed my arms, knocked away my sword, held me pinned. Obilin smiled, and seemed no more ugly now than at any other time I had seen that smile.

"No chances this time," Obilin grated. The light mood vanished. The chatter was gone now; he let the hatred show. "Thanks to you, Rikardon, I've lost a very comfortable position in Eddarta. Oh, Indomel still thinks I work for him—that I came here on his behalf, looking for the lady. But I didn't come all this way only to take you back to Eddarta. Oh, no. Not at all."

He moved closer.

"*This*," Obilin said, stabbing the air for emphasis "is *private*. I knew when I left that I wouldn't be going back. That's why I brought *this* along."

He turned the sword; lamplight gleamed against its silvery edges.

"Worfit isn't a selfish man," Obilin continued. "In fact, I find him quite easy to work with. When he saw me, and heard my story, he agreed that I had at least as fair a claim on your death as he does.

"Do you want to hear the bargain, Rikardon?" he asked, his voice getting hoarser and rougher as he approached me. "I had the sword. I traded it to him for your life, on condition that I could first kill you with it. And it *is* a bargain, Rikardon. Your life isn't worth a fleabite. Especially right now."

He had come so close that I could see the slight rise of the tissue that formed the scars on his face, smell barut on his breath.

"Hold him steady!" he commanded my captors, and lifted Rika over his head.

I was desert-hardened and mad as hell at this little, mangled man who had made so much trouble for us. I was desperate to survive because, without me, I knew Tarani would die. (I didn't have to fear she'd be hurt in the way Obilin so badly wanted to hurt her—I knew she'd find a way to die.) Rage, a living and separate thing, took over my body and fought for my life.

I made such a show of struggling that both men clutched my arms tightly. Then, as the sword started down, I jumped, folded, and kicked—straight into Obilin's face. The sword came down through the air in front of me. I had jumped off-center, to throw my weight against one man; the movement pulled the other man around in front of me. Rika sliced through the back of his calf, and he screamed, hanging on to my arm with one hand and clawing at my face with the other.

Obilin had recovered and was shouting at him to move out of the way. I shifted my weight again and shoved the three of us into Obilin. We all went down in a furious tangle. I was closer to the top. I placed some hurtful punches and pulled myself out of it. I grabbed the table—Pornon was watching from halfway up the stairs—and tipped it over on the struggling group.

For a few seconds I debated trying to sort Rika out of the mess, but I couldn't spare the time. Obilin was driving the other two off of him with fists and sword and curses; he would be free in seconds.

I ran toward the door.

Two of the bar clientele were picking up Tarani, with a studied indifference about where they put their hands.

I stiff-armed into them, knocking them back against the wall. I pulled Tarani away from them and fought the blind rage that was urging me to kill this pair.

The real enemy's behind you, I told myself. *These guys—it was nothing personal; she's just a woman to them.*

It was a triumph of rationality that I reached for my dagger and cut open Tarani's money pouch. Coins spilled and scattered on the floor. The men against the wall and in the bar's doorway leaned forward. It was a considerable sum; Zefra had been generous.

"I just bought five minutes head start," I said, ducking down to lift Tarani in a poorly balanced fireman's carry. I backed out the door, holding the dagger awkwardly in front of me.

"You want the little guy killed?" the man nearest the door said.

I looked through the doorway at Obilin, who was standing, holding the steel sword. With that, with his fighting skill, with his fury, he'd have a chance, even against these odds.

"Use your own judgment," I said, and ran for it.

18

I ran all night, only pausing to rearrange Tarani's limp form across my aching shoulders. At dawn I dragged Tarani into a rocky hollow away from the road, and slept fitfully for a couple of hours. I jumped awake, startled from a grim and fading dream. Tarani lay peacefully beside me, her breathing disturbingly sharp and shallow.

She should be awake by now, I thought. *Obilin must have given her a concussion—and that bouncing last night couldn't have helped her.* Panic took hold as I touched her face. *At least she's breathing,* I tried to reassure myself. *We must have a sizable lead by now. We'll stay put; I'll let her rest; she'll be all right.*

I poured some water on my scarf and bathed her face, then moved my fingers gently over her skull. The size of the knot at the base of her skull frightened me, and I wished for Tarani's healing skill.

We stayed there most of the day, except for graduated movement as the shade pattern around the tallest rocks changed. I dozed fitfully, but even asleep, I was waiting for the sound of a group of men coming up the trail. Never had I felt such appreciation for Tarani's link with Lonna. The bird appeared now and then to hoot mournfully near her mistress, but she left without giving me any information. She could speak only to Tarani.

It was nearly dusk when Tarani made a sound. I scrabbled over the dusty rock to crouch beside her, resisting the urge to pull her up into my arms. Her eyes opened. "What happened?" she whispered. She pulled one of her hands away from mine and touched the back of her head. "Ouch." Then she looked me straight in the eyes and said: "Obilin."

I nodded.

"Is he dead this time?" she asked.

"I don't know," I said, and told her what had happened.

"It's money well spent," she said, when she'd heard it all. "I hope they tore the fleason to pieces."

Tarani must have seen how her savagery shocked me. "I think of Vasklar," she explained more gently. "How he will feel when he knows where his good efforts have led."

"I know," I said, sharing her bitterness.

She looked around at the rocks. "Where are we?"

"Just east of the Zantril," I said. "I was afraid to take you into the pass unconscious."

"How long?"

"We've been here for most of a day," I said.

"Oh, Rikardon—I'm sorry I have held you back. If Obilin is not dead—if Worfit knows you were in Chizan—"

"Lonna's not too far away," I said. "Can you find out if somebody's following us?"

She closed her eyes. The bird swooped down and settled on a boulder near her, took off, returned. Tarani opened her eyes, and the pain in them shocked me.

"It must be the blow," she said in explanation. "It hurts to speak to Lonna. But it hurts more to hear what she has to tell. A party of twenty men, wearing backpacks, is coming from Chizan, no more than an hour away. There are two men in the lead. One is Obilin, I'm sure, from your description. The other is not much taller, but wide and muscular..."

"That's Worfit," I confirmed, and thought furiously. "Can we sit tight and let them pass us?"

"I do not think so," she said. "Lonna's picture shows the main group moving at a steady pace, with others off on either side, searching." She gripped my upper arms. "Help me up; we must get moving," she said.

I pulled her, slowly, into a sitting position. She no more than got up there than she was pushing me away. She turned her body full against the shade rock and lay there retching for what seemed an endless time.

"You can't travel, Tarani—that blow *hurt* you."

"I *must* travel," she gasped. "Help me."

I did, hating the grayness in her face, hurting for her. I pulled her to her feet and held her around her waist. I dragged her the first few steps, but then she was walking on her own, leaning on me for support. We paused twice for retching spasms; then they went away. At the entrance to the Zantril, Tarani sent Lonna out again. The troop was still on our trail, gaining but not quickly. They had decided, apparently, that endurance was more important than speed.

They may be right, I thought, as we clambered down the steep slope into the dust-blown chasm that was the Zantril crossing. In spite of the scarf covering Tarani's face, the dust made her cough, and that made her head hurt more. Lonna had to fend for herself this trip; I saw her once, through the stinging dust, struggling in the wind.

It had taken three healthy people twenty hours to walk through this pass on my last trip. This time, I thought the Zantril was endless. I wasn't sure what day or hour it was when I topped the high point that marked the other end of the pass. I was staggering under Tarani's weight—she had passed out again, several hours ago, and she had never looked really well.

I staggered down the outer slope, relieved beyond words to see the scrubby bushes clinging stubbornly to the hillside. I found a fairly shady spot sheltered from sight of the road, lowered Tarani to the ground, and stretched out beside her. Obilin and Molik notwithstanding, we needed some rest. I drew in deep lungfuls of air, grateful that it didn't taste of dust. After a while, I slept.

Tarani shook me awake. I resisted, clinging to the dream.

I had four legs, very satisfying claws, and tawny fur. The female was a musky presence, a pleasant nuisance with her fussy searching for the right lair. Any defensible place would do for me—a cave, a hollowed-out thicket. But she sniffed and pawed and dug. A nuisance.

I reached far forward with my front legs, dug my claws into the leaf-covered ground, slowly pulled my back out straight, and stretched my back legs one at a time. The sweet smell of the disturbed leaves drifted up to me. The female was off to my left. Water lay before me. I could hear it rushing over the rocks, smell its coolness . . .

"Keeshah!" I said, sitting bolt upright. I turned to Tarani, who was looking better, and grabbed her arms. "It wasn't a dream," I said. "It was Keeshah. We're still linked, somehow."

"Rikardon," Tarani said, breaking gently from my hold, "I have an idea."

I stood up and looked northward. "That's the Valley of the Sha'um," I said, pointing to the northwest, to the left of the dark blotch on the landscape that was called—for reasons of appearance, I supposed—the Well of Darkness.

"We're closer here, Tarani. That must make a difference." I turned to her, excited. I grabbed her, hugged her. "Keeshah's still with me!" I shouted.

"And Obilin and Worfit are getting closer!" she yelled against my shoulder. She pushed me away, closed her eyes and pressed her hands to her temples. "Listen to me, Rikardon," she said, after she had taken a few deep breaths. "Lonna woke me with her screeching. Obilin and Worfit are barely an hour short of this end of the pass. Let us send Lonna to Thagorn. We may be able to make it to Relenor safely, and wait there for Thymas."

I forced my mind away from my welcome "dream" to consider Tarani's plan. There was no doubt Thymas would come. If it weren't enough that Tarani asked Thymas, through Lonna, for help, he would be bound through his oath to his father to obey the Captain's orders. But there were bigger questions.

Did we have time to wait for their help, even considering the speed of a hundred men riding a hundred sha'um?

When I'd been named Captain, I had told the Sharith that it wasn't time, yet, for them to go into action. Was it time now, only because the danger was personal to me?

Lastly, Obilin knew we had connections in Thagorn, and might suspect we were doing exactly what Tarani planned. He would hardly be inclined to wait around for a fang-and-claw army to descend on Relenor.

"Do you really think the 'sanctuary' of a Refreshment House will stop Obilin or Worfit?" I asked.

"Perhaps not them," Tarani said. "Obilin, I know, is too determined to reach us. But the other men—the tradition will mean something to them. Obilin and Worfit will have to come in alone, or force or convince the others to violate the tradition of the Fa'aldu. It will buy us time."

"At what cost to the Fa'aldu?" I demanded, and looked northward again.

"If not the Refreshment House," she pleaded, "let us at least start for Thagorn, and send Lonna ahead. We can stay out of Obilin's reach long enough for Thymas to bring the Sharith."

I pulled Tarani down into a sitting position and faced her. I gathered my thoughts and tried to calm the growing excitement. I knew what I had to do, and I wanted her with me, not out of loyalty, but with full understanding.

"It's no use to send Lonna to Thagorn," I said. "It's too far; she's too tired. We'll go north, into the Valley."

She started to protest, but I hurried on. "It's not as impractical as it seems," I said. "There's a passage through the west wall of the Valley. It's a hard crossing, but we can make it—it leads to Alkhum, a little town not far from Raithskar."

She studied my face.

"Do you forget that I know something of sha'um?" she asked quietly. "They will kill us if we invade their Valley."

"Keeshah is there!" I said fiercely. "He'll let us through."

"But no one else will be able to enter," she mused. "And the Fa'aldu will not be endangered by those who follow us."

She put her hand on my cheek.

"It is logical, my love—a measured chance. But I see the truth in your face. You wish to do this only to be with Keeshah again."

I nodded, knowing that the decision was now hers, terrified that she would refuse me.

"It is reason enough," she said.

She didn't say what we both know, I thought gratefully as we pulled out the last of our food and munched while we ran down the slope, aiming northwest. *She didn't mention that Obilin and Worfit are too close. The odds for survival in any direction are rotten.*

I hurt all over, and I knew she was even worse off. Her face was set in a steady grimace—easier than flinching with every step. We heard, faintly, the shouting behind us as the troop topped the rise and saw us moving across the scantily covered bottom of the slope. We didn't even look back.

This could be the end of the quest, I thought. *She knows it, too. That's why she accepted my need for Keeshah so readily.*

Thoughts of the big cat called back the "dream". *It was so real, so true*, I told myself. *It had to be coming through our link. But why haven't I felt it before this? Distance can't have that much to do with it—we left Keeshah two days out of Eddarta, and I could speak to him as easily as if I were riding him.*

There was one aspect of the "dream" that I hadn't mentioned to Tarani, and I didn't want to remember now, but it seemed important. *Keeshah didn't remember me*, I admitted. *And he didn't know I was there.*

He must have been with me all the time, I thought, *but I've only now realized he's there. It can't be that the link suddenly came back—I would have felt it, the way I felt it when I thought it left. He just ...shut down this part of his life for a while.*

I wonder if that's what happens to all of the sha'um, I thought. *For their time in the Valley, they're just smart animals for a while, intent on the biological business of continuing their species. It's an entirely different life for them, one they don't remember when they come back into the world they share with their riders.*

Tarani and I were keeping a decent pace. Our lead over the men behind us shrank more slowly than I had been expecting. They hadn't been pushing as hard or as long as we had—but neither had they been toughened, recently, by a run across the Strofaan. They had had a reasonably soft life in Chizan, and we had been on the road, not counting our eight-day rest at Stomestad, for more than a month.

My mind stayed with the memory of Keeshah in the Valley, both because it was my only real contact with him since he had left us in the desert and because of the puzzle the vision presented. *Why would I become aware of the link now?* I wondered. *Or at all, for that matter? Tarani said the rest of the Sharith never had a clue about what happened in the Valley.*

Excitement gripped me. *But nobody else has the same kind of link as Keeshah's and mine. Ours is a different quality, not just communication, but a lifesharing—motivations, emotions—*

*Emotions—*I missed my step and fell flat on my face, skidding in the sand.

Tarani was beside me, helping me up. Her eyes were curious, but she didn't waste breath asking questions.

Me, I was busy kicking myself for not seeing the truth sooner.

Keeshah goes into his animal state, I reasoned. *The link is still open, though neither one of us is really aware of it. He's troubled by the most powerful emotion he's ever felt, the need to mate. And I can't think clearly because that need is affecting me, unrecognized, through the link. He finds his mate, and courts her, as cats do, with teasing and passion ...*

I groaned inwardly, remembering a roll down a hillside, and the need that had overtaken me then.

No wonder Tarani couldn't think straight either, I thought. *She was trying to deal with a man who was half animal.*

141

I can blame Keeshah, now, for the fierceness of what happened in Carn's cellar. I thought my release had cleared my head—but now I think it was Keeshah's. That must have been the moment when he mated with the female.

As desperate as our situation was just then, I still wanted to laugh as I thought: *It's a good thing Tarani and I were in a private place when Keeshah got laid.*

But if I give Keeshah credit for the passion, don't I have to give him credit for the feelings, too? Is what I feel for Tarani all mine, or part Keeshah's feeling for his lady?

It didn't take long to put that worry to rest. All I had to do was call up the "dream" again. The quality of Keeshah's relationship to the female was strictly on an animal level—a good-humored tolerance, respect for their shared purpose, devotion to the concept of family. Not only was there no trace of the tenderness and joy I felt when I looked at Tarani, but I could find no similarity between what Keeshah felt for the female and what I knew he felt for me.

Well, maybe one similarity, I admitted. *I've felt that "good-humored tolerance" from him a time or two.*

"Rikardon," Tarani panted.

Awakened from my reverie, I realized that my sides were beginning to hurt and that I, as well as Tarani, was laboring for breath.

I checked my inner awareness. Several hours had run by while I had been engrossed in my discovery of the existing Keeshah/Rikardon mindlink. I looked back in sudden panic, but the flapping scarfs and puffing dust of the troop of men seemed no closer to us.

"Something's wrong," I said, and looked ahead of us, expecting to see the thickening line of green that would mark the beginning of the forested area in which the sha'um lived. It should have been straight ahead, Obilin and Worfit straight behind us. The line was there, all right, but off to our left, with the running men edging up between it and us.

I wasted breath and a few precious seconds swearing at myself. I had been preoccupied, running automatically, peripherally aware of our lead distance but blithely assuming the direction was right. We had been skillfully herded away from our original goal—no doubt at the instigation of Worfit, who knew of my sha'um connection—and were aimed due north now, directly toward the Well of Darkness.

I studied distances, did some figuring, and came up with disaster if we tried to cut across the path of Worfit's men.

My link to Keeshah is unique, I told myself. I knew it was a long shot—I had seen into his mind, seen the blank place that had once been his friend Rikardon—but I put a part of my mind into gear, screaming "*HELP, KEESHAH!*" at full volume.

It wasn't just his help I wanted. It was his awareness, a return of the closeness I had missed for so long.

But I couldn't dwell on what seemed our slimmest chance. I clutched my aching sides and looked ahead, searching for some hope in the landscape.

I see now why they call it a well, I thought. We had topped a sharp ridge that seemed to circle the huge, spreading darkness. I stumbled to a stop, less from fatigue than from curiosity and amazement. We were looking into an inverted cone of land perhaps a mile wide. Another step would start us down the side of the cone, which was covered with pale, crumbly-looking rock dotted, here and there, with chunks of gleaming black. Some two hundred yards deep in the cone drifted a smoggy-looking light fog. It lay across the "well", a light swirling motion suggesting a subtle turbulence. It formed a transparent layer that truncated the cone; we could see the ground clearly enough through its edges.

But if we looked down, toward the center of the cone, that transparent layer merged into a darker one, then one even blacker. We couldn't see the ground, even at the edge of the fog, more than four hundred yards straight down.

"Well of Darkness," I panted. "Perfect name for it."

"I've heard of it all my life," Tarani said, "but I had no idea it was this big." She looked back over her shoulder. "We cannot stay here, Rikardon."

I took her hand and started down the steep slope. It was treacherous going, with the gravel-size rocks sliding out from under our feet with every other step. I had to let go her hand and use both mine to keep upright. Luckily, the slope wasn't perfectly smooth, but stairstepped with uneven ledges.

"Call Lonna," I ordered, a little awed that Tarani had followed me unquestioningly. "They're expecting us to turn aside here, and think they can cut us off then between here and the Valley. We can't cross this—that stuff has to be poisonous—but we can hold our breath and take short dips

143

into it. Lonna can guide us, tell us when it's safe to come up for air."

"They will line the rim and wait for us," she said.

"Not the eastern rim," I panted, "the side away from the Valley. They won't expect that. We ought to be able to work our way around to the north, and climb out the other side. By then, I'm hoping they'll assume we're dead. If not—we'll at least have surprise on our side, and that may give us enough of a head start to reach the Valley."

We had clambered down until breathing was becoming difficult, and I realized that the top layer of gas was even more transparent, once we were inside it.

That makes things harder, I thought, dragging Tarani back up the slope a ways. *For this to work, we've got to go deep enough to be obscured from sight. I thought this layer might be breathable, but from its taste and smell, it's richly layered with sulfur. It's going to take all our breath-holding time just to dip down to the heavier layers and get back up in time to breathe again.*

I could hear men shouting to one another. They would be standing on the rim in minutes, and if they saw which direction we were taking, we'd be trapped for sure.

"Is Lonna ready?" I asked.

"Yes," Tarani said.

"Aren't you going to tell me this is a crazy idea?" I asked.

"You know that already," she said.

She stumbled, caught my arm for support, smiled. I kissed her, lightly.

"Let's go," I said.

We took deep breaths and slid and scrambled down the slope toward the darkness. As we moved deeper into the relatively clear top layer, my eyes began to sting and water, and I was already wanting my next breath. When we dipped into the murkiness below, I had to close my eyes to protect them, and we felt our way deeper.

Tarani tugged at my hand and we struggled back up the slope. We both gave out and gasped for breath a little too soon. The gas stung my eyes and burned my lungs. Tarani's coughing told me she was having the same sort of trouble. We crawled higher, breathing heavily when the air was cleaner and lying still for several minutes. When I felt I could move again, I looked around. We had been traveling east-ward on the zig and the zag of our short trip, and were a good distance from our starting point. We lay in clear view, should anyone be looking—but the men who had followed us were stationing themselves along the western rim, and looking straight down.

I felt a surge of hope.

"They're not looking for us," I gasped to Tarani. "I don't think we need to go quite so deep."

The ground trembled slightly, and Tarani jerked up on her elbows.

"What was that?" she cried.

I wondered what the Gandalarans believed the Well of Darkness to be. I found I couldn't tell Tarani what I—what Ricardo—knew it was. Gandaresh had no vocabulary equivalent for *volcano*.

Unless you count "Well of Darkness" as a generic, as well as specific, term, I thought. *This seems to be the only volcano in Gandalara, and a mildly active one, if that ground tremor is any indication.*

I ignored Tarani's question and started breathing deeply, getting ready for the next stage of the trip.

I also checked the volume of my SOS signal to Keeshah, and turned it up a notch.

19

We had dipped down into that stinging, cloying mess of gases three times more before I finally figured out why we were making such good distance.

"Lonna's watching us and giving you directions, isn't she?" I said.

Tarani only nodded through a spasm of coughing. She looked as bad as I felt.

There didn't seem to be one square inch of surface, inside of me or outside, that wasn't burning from exposure to the gas or stinging from scraping on the rocks *and* exposure to the gas. I looked westward, but my watering eyes couldn't see the opposite rim very clearly.

"I'd guess we're pretty close to the easternmost point of the rim, directly opposite the group watching for us," I said. "Will you ask Lonna if that's right?"

She closed her eyes, then nodded.

"Then I think we can quit trying to breathe soup," I said. "We can climb up and work around the rest of the way on the far side of the rim."

"Thank Zanek for that!" Tarani gasped, and we started the treacherous climb.

We moved slowly. I felt weak as a baby—I doubted I would have been able to make another trip into that smelly darkness, anyway. Our clothes were covered with a sooty dust that helped them blend in with the color of the slope, so I didn't worry too much about the long periods we lay still, totally exposed to anyone who might be looking our way.

When we got close enough to touch the weathered edge of rock that marked the rim, the ground trembled again, and Tarani whimpered. Lonna swept down from the sky, concern for Tarani's distress drawing her. She hovered about twenty feet above us.

Lonna screeched. It was a blood-freezing cry of pain. My eyes were blurred, but I could hear her wingbeat falter and stop. When she hit the ground close to us and started to skid down the slope, I had no trouble distinguishing the dark red stain spreading slowly through the whiteness of her feathers, or seeing the dagger hilt at the center of the stain.

Tarani moaned and crawled over to Lonna's body, catching it by a wingtip before it could slide down into the well. She hugged the bird tight against her chest, rolled to her back and lay still.

"Tarani," I whispered. Her head turned toward me, but her eyes were blank. Utterly blank.

"*Obilin!*" I screamed, and launched myself over the rim of the crater. "This is the end of it, you bastard! You hear me, Obilin?"

I found my feet and stared around in a wild fury, blinking away the tears that were washing the last of the stinging smog out of my eyes. Obilin waited for me not ten yards away. Small drifts of dust in the air told me he had just now slid back down from this side of the rim.

"This will be the end of it indeed," Obilin said in his damaged voice. "I have not made the error, this time, of trusting others. You always manage to use the others against me. But now——" He pulled the steel sword from his baldric and gestured, inviting me downslope. "We're alone. Worfit's a good man—he followed my instructions to the letter, allowing you to think you had fooled us while I crept along after that idiotic bird. But he has sworn not to interfere—unless I fail. And Tarani no longer has my interest, Rikardon. You. Your death. That is all I care about now."

I drew my sword and moved cautiously down the slope. The red heat of rage had coalesced into a white-hot point of hatred that left me room to think and plan.

This territory is in his favor, I calculated. *Lots of room for those quick and fancy moves of his. That's got to be the first priority—limit his mobility.*

We circled. He lunged in, swung an overhand blow which I blocked, then leaped back again. The edge of my bronze sword was no longer smooth.

For the first time, I was *facing* Rika, rather than wielding it.

That's another point on his side, I conceded, then warned myself: *He's got the advantage with the steel sword; don't double it by letting it rattle you.*

He came in again, swinging low this time. I blocked, whirled, swung—but he had danced away.

Remember, I thought, *offense is his strength, defense his weaker skill*.

I pressed him then, slashing and swinging, forcing him to use his sword instead of his feet. I yelled with every stroke. I outweighed the man, and I was stronger. Fury had restored the energy that had been nearly totally drained only moments before. I beat Obilin back, not caring for the nicks and dents in my own sword. He was quick. I couldn't touch him.

When he realized I was forcing him up the slope toward the rim of the Well, he changed tactics. He started moving faster, slashing in at me between his blocks. Rika was no more than a blur in his hands. We were at a standoff, not moving in either direction.

I let my guard down on the right, hoping I could time it correctly. He lunged in, Rika swinging into my side; I jumped to my left as I blocked. Obilin saw the opening I had left him, and whirled to jump downslope.

I had my dagger in my left hand. As he turned, I jabbed at him, catching the back of his right thigh.

He fell, rather than jumped, down the slope, and I was right on his heels. He rolled to his back and braced Rika in front of his face. I pressed my sword down on Rika, straining my strength against Obilin's, and jabbed again with the dagger. This time it lodged in his side.

Obilin grunted, and the steel sword moved fractionally closer to his body under the pressure of my sword. The little man's good eye, unchanged by the scarred skin all around it, looked at me from above the sword with the same expression of insolent challenge that I had always seen in there.

"You can't win," Obilin gasped in a broken whisper. "Worfit will finish it—for me and for himself."

"But you, Obilin," I said fiercely. "You have failed."

"No," he gasped, taking in a ragged breath. "I haven't killed you, Rikardon, but I have marked you. You and the lady will not soon forget me." His scarred face rearranged itself into the familiar, sneering smile. "It is a . . . satisfactory revenge."

I gritted my teeth and, with a terrible joy, I jerked the dagger in Obilin's side upward to rip a long, bloody gash through clothes and flesh. Rika snapped downward, its tip grating against the rocky hillside.

I threw down the battered bronze sword, picked up Rika with a feeling of meeting an old, much-missed friend, and

148

slipped the steel sword through my baldric. I looked down at Obilin and knew he had been right—his death would leave a deeper scar in me than any I had given him. Later, I might examine the pleasure I had taken in killing Obilin, and judge how it had changed me. Now, I only felt relief, and a sudden return of fear.

I scrambled over the rim of the well down to Tarani. I slapped her lightly; she roused and followed me back up the slope, still clutching Lonna's still form.

She was in touch with Lonna when Obilin killed the bird, I thought, and felt a pang of loss when I thought of the bird's death.

I heard shouting, and looked up to see men running around the rim of the Well, and I felt my last hope give way. The fight with Obilin had taken my last reserves. I was shaking from the inside out, barely able to hold to Tarani's hand.

I pulled Tarani into my arms, holding her and Lonna in what I believed to be our last farewell. I pressed my cheek against Tarani's and reached out with my mind.

Keeshah, I thought. *If only I could ride you one more time . . .*

I COME!

It was like a shout echoing through a long corridor, at first, a sense of tremendous volume at the source but only faintly heard. Then, as if it had been beyond a barrier and the barrier suddenly dissolved, it was clear and close, the old link re-established.

I come, Keeshsah said again, the thought more normal in tone. *Close. Do not die.*

I started to laugh, but my lungs still burned and the effort trailed off into coughing.

Die? I echoed. *Who, me?*

I gripped Rika, drawing some confidence merely from holding the steel sword once more, and faced south. Six to eight men were racing around the rim toward us, only two or three minutes away. I recognized the squat figure of Worfit in the van of the group.

When I glanced northward, however, I was greeted with a familiar, cherished sight—a lean, tawny figure streaking toward us at full speed.

Keeshsah reached us a few precious seconds before Worfit, who skidded to a stop when he saw Keeshah. He turned to give orders, and discovered that he was alone. The other men had stopped several yards behind him. They replied to the roguelord's yelling with shaking heads and a general movement backward.

I was aware of Worfit and his men only marginally. I left Tarani to fling my arms around Keeshah, and I rubbed my face into the fur behind his massive jaw, delighting in the feel and smell of the sha'um. He sidestepped, dragging me with him, and lifted and ducked his head to take full advantage of the rubbing motion.

We were together again, the mindlink clear and sweet, no thought of the past weeks intruding except in our awareness that this was a reunion. Our minds achieved the special and elemental joining that Keeshah and I had shared so often, and emotions rocketed through us—the fierce tenderness of our friendship, the exhilaration of recovered loss, needs and joys and the exquisite reality of being together—until their intensity overwhelmed us and the merging dissolved.

Go, Keeshah urged. *Not safe here.*

I looked around. Worfit had gone back to his men and was literally driving them toward us with his hands and sword. They were moving reluctantly, but beginning to feel the confidence of their greater number as more came around the rim to join the group.

Keeshah crouched down and I pulled Tarani toward him. She had remained standing where I had left her, showing little sign that she knew what was going on, but she paused near Keeshah's head.

"Sha'um," she murmured, and reached out to stroke back the fur between Keeshah's eyes.

The cat folded back his ears and gently nosed the bloody carcass in Tarani's arms.

Bird gone, he said to me. *Sorry.*

"We have to hurry," I told Tarani gently. She nodded, her eyes still distant, and mounted Keeshah. The girl still held Lonna, and I couldn't bring myself to argue with her. I mounted second, and Keeshah surged to his feet while the group of men closed in cautiously.

Worfit had directed them well; they had nearly circled us. A single gap remained—due north. I spared one second to look directly at the roguelord and laugh, then Keeshah carried us away from the Well of Darkness.

I didn't have to tell Keeshah where to go. In that moment

150

of close sharing, he had learned directly of our needs, and I had seen his. He took us into the Valley of the Sha'um.

I woke with the roar of a sha'um's fighting challenge vibrating in my ears.

Keeshah! I called, disoriented for a moment by the darkness and the odd smell.

Stay out of the way, Keeshah ordered me—and memory returned.

The big cat had brought us across the remaining desert into the thick forest of the Valley which seemed, topologically, to be less an actual valley than a triangle of forested area bounded on the north by the Great Wall and on the West by the Morkadahl Mountains, through which ran the Alkhum Pass. He had threaded his way through the flatter area of the triangle and into the foothills of the Morkadahls, where briars and viney growth entangled the trunks of the tallest trees in Gandalara. He had shown us the entrance to a cavelike hollow in the snarled vines above a small clearing. Tarani and I had crept into its shadowy interior and collapsed.

I recognized it now. It had a musky, earthy smell that wasn't the least unpleasant. We had slept on a cushion of leaves and pungent needles, and air and light penetrated the interwoven vines around us.

This is Keeshah's lair, I thought. *He brought us home. But what's going on outside?*

I shuffled through the leaves to the shaded circle that was the lair's entrance, nearly hidden from the meadow below it by a stand of young trees. I found a place from which I could see into the meadow.

Keeshah was there, facing down a smaller, gray sha'um. Around them were six sha'um I could see, probably more waiting in the shadowy forest. But all the rest seemed content to watch.

The gray lunged at Keeshah, and the two cats clinched briefly then broke apart, snarling at one another. There was blood on the gray's muzzle and along Keeshah's foreleg, but neither wound looked serious. The smaller sha'um closed in again. Keeshah wrestled him to the ground, lay with the gray pinned beneath him, snarling at the others. The smaller sha'um roared and twitched, waited, struggled again, then lay quiescent.

In a swift movement, Keeshah released the smaller male

151

and backed cautiously toward the lair. Another male, bigger than the gray and marked with a nearly white spot along one side of his muzzle, stepped forward.

Keeshah, what's happening? I asked, but was ignored.

The two sha'um went into crouch, the fur behind their heads lifting into manes and their tails whipping slowly back and forth. After they had each roared a challenge, their voices were reduced to muttering, deep-throated growls that raised my headfur. The other cats moved back, giving them room . . .

And a third sha'um entered the clearing, seeming to appear out of nowhere.

"A female," Tarani said from beside me, startling me. The vacant look had left her eyes. "She's Keeshah's mate."

I didn't wonder, then, how Tarani knew that—I was much too glad to see her responding and recovering from the initial shock of Lonna's death. And I was engrossed in what was happening in the clearing.

The female was marked for the forest rather than the desert. Her coat was brindled in browns and grays, and her fur seemed thicker than Keeshah's. She made no move to join the fight, but walked over to Keeshah and rubbed the side of her jaw along his back. She paused to look at the other male, but made no threatening gestures. Instead she came slowly up the hill—right toward us.

Tarani stood up and went to meet her.

They assessed each other warily, the pale-skinned woman and the dark-furred cat. Tarani stretched out her hand, palm up. The female stretched her neck and dipped her head to sniff delicately at Tarani's hand. I saw the girl's neck muscles twitch, but she held her arm steady. The sha'um's nose touched Tarani's palm, jerked back, then pressed in again.

Tarani brought up her other hand slowly and touched the female sha'um's chin. The cat flinched slightly, then stood quivering as the girl's hand moved slowly, smoothing back the fur on the cat's throat.

The sha'um's ears, folded back when she had approached Tarani, relaxed forward under the girl's caress. A sound from the clearing snapped them back again, and the female whirled away from Tarani. Tail thickened and neckfur bristling, the brindled female answered the challenge of the white-faced male and stalked down to stand beside Keeshah, making it clear that he would have to take on both of them.

I'd had enough exposure to sha'um to know they weren't dumb.

The white-faced male backed down. He retreated into the circle of males.

Keeshah took a step forward and called his challenge again, but there weren't any takers. The ring of sha'um shuffled backward until the sha'um seemed merely to fade away into the shadows of the forest.

I discovered I was trembling. I moved to stand beside Tarani, touching her elbow to let her know I was there. She jumped, and looked at me with shining eyes.

"Rikardon," she breathed. "We are linked, the female and I. We spoke today for the first time, but she has been with me before now." She spread her arms. "In my dreams I have seen this forest, moved through it on four legs, hunted glith on the plain, wild vlek in the hills above the Valley. Many different dreams, so scattered and seemingly unconnected that their strangeness frightened me."

Tarani put her hand on my arm, and spoke tenderly.

"Now I understand more than my own dreams, Rikardon. I have learned what you and Keeshah shared, and how devastating its loss must have been for you. Your link with Keeshah—?"

"It's back," I said. She smiled and squeezed my arm. "It never left, really," I told her. "It just went inactive because coming to the Valley was a biological priority. When I needed Keeshah more than his mate did, our link came back to the conscious level."

I turned to watch Keeshah and his mate approach us. I scratched Keeshah in his favorite place, just behind the heavy jaw bone. Tarani touched the female more tentatively but, clearly, with no less joy. Keeshah's mate accepted Tarani's attention awkwardly as woman and sha'um began to get acquainted.

"You said you spoke to her," I reminded Tarani. "What did she say?"

Tarani laughed.

"No words," she said. "And not just pictures, either, the way it was with Lonna." Her laughter died, and her hands clenched in the female's fur, causing the sha'um to sidestep uncertainly. Tarani recovered, and resumed stroking the cat. "Not even you, my beautiful Yayshah," she said softly, "can take Lonna's place in my heart."

"Yayshah?" I repeated.

"Yes, I have given her that name," Tarani said, pulling herself away from her grief. "As I say, there were no words between us, only emotions and, well, meanings." She shrugged. "You understand what I mean better than I, I expect. Surprise at discovering our link, and—after a moment of hesitation—a sweet, uncomplicated delight. Then she asked me if you were my mate." She smiled, but looked at Yayshah as she said: "I said yes, of course."

"Is that why she joined the fight?" I asked Tarani. "Was Keeshah defending me?"

"I think so," Tarani said. "Why does that surprise you?"

"I figured he was fighting for you," I said. "When I—when Markasset came here as a boy and linked with Keeshah, the other sha'um accepted me, but you're totally a stranger to them."

Keeshah, apparently, had been following my thoughts.

Cub was one of them, Keeshah told me. *I am a stranger.*

I felt the irony, and Keeshah's regret, in his acceptance of being an outsider among his own kind.

I have done that to you, Keeshah, I said, but the sha'um forestalled what would have been an apology that would, in any case, have been insincere. I couldn't wish Keeshah back to his natural state if it meant sacrificing his link with me.

Others wanted you for food, Keeshah said, radiating contempt. *Female, too.*

"Yayshah?" I said out loud. Tarani looked at me. "Keeshah says the other sha'um, including Yayshah, wanted me for dinner—or," I added, looking around the clearing and listening to my inner awareness, "breakfast."

Tarani stroked the female in silence for a moment, frowning with concentration.

"I think—it seems that wasn't it at all," Tarani said. "She had been hunting, and returned to her lair to find that Keeshah had appropriated it for us. She resented it, but she had a vague sense of her linkage with me, and tried to get inside to see us. Keeshah drove her off, and she waited until he was occupied to return. That gesture we saw—the way she rubbed his back?"

I nodded.

"She was telling him—and the others—that she's his mate and on his side." Tarani shook her head. "Rikardon, how is it they speak so clearly to us, but cannot talk to one another?"

154

"I'm beginning to have a theory about that," I said. "Keeshah says he's an outsider, now, and I think it has more to do with our link than it does with his long absence from the Valley. That 'dream' I had of him, just after we came through the Zantril Pass—I saw him the way the others must always be. He was . . . only an animal, with a native but largely inactive intelligence. When a sha'um links with a man, it gives him a way to use that intelligence, it teaches him how to reason, educates him, if you will."

"So he speaks to man and sha'um in the language each will understand," Tarani said, scratching behind Yayshah's ear with more assurance. "You came here as a child, Rikardon, and bonded with a young sha'um. But I—and Yayshah—how can it have happened?"

I cleared my throat, but found I couldn't say what I was thinking.

Tarani smiled. "Carn's cellar," she said. "It occurred to me, too, that if you were linked to Keeshah at the moment of his mating with Yayshah, our—uh—" She broke off, blushing, then continued. "But I am sure Yayshah was with me even before then, Rikardon. On the hillside—remember?—I wanted you, lured you, fought you, and still, throughout it all, wanted you. When I laughed—the sound of it frightened me. I felt I couldn't control my own feelings. She was with me then, Rikardon."

Tarani left Yayshah and came to stand in front of me.

"But her influence was only in the character of my actions," Tarani said, "She added an extra dimension to a passion that was already my own. Knowing that about Yayshah and myself—it tells me something of you, as well."

I took her hands.

"I don't have answers, Tarani, only opinions. Keeshah and I share a mindlink that is special, even among Sharith. You're strongly mindgifted. I'm not saying your power, by itself, set up the link with Yayshah—but it might have made you susceptible. A compulsion is direct mind-to-mind communication of a sort, isn't it? When I came here, it was Keeshah who first spoke to me—perhaps it's always like that, and the boys who don't return from the Valley are unlucky enough to choose cubs who aren't capable of the—what? Curiosity? Initiative? Perhaps they just don't have the native skill at all.

"Whatever it is, Yayshah has it. When she formed the mate

bond with Keeshah, who was mind-bonded to me . . ."

"But, I told you," Tarani protested, "that it was present before . . ."

"Not before *we* established our 'mate bond'," I interrupted her. "That happened long before we arrived at Carn's cellar, Tarani. At least, for me it did."

"Then it must be the same for sha'um," Tarani said, smiling up at me. "It is the act of *choosing* a mate, not of *possessing* him, which forms the bond."

20

Tarani and I found a beautiful spot to wash off the grime, if not the memory, of our ordeal in the Well of Darkness. One of the several small streams which fed the lush growth of the Valley tumbled down a brief cataract and changed direction suddenly, leaving at one edge a small, rock-lined bay of less turbulent water. We came upon it suddenly while following a stand of brambly berry vines, eating as we walked. We weren't the least surprised to find that the bank was free of undergrowth, green and soft with a springy grass-like ground cover. We had already discovered that these hills in the Valley were an endless and delightful mixture of impassable briars, sunny meadows, and open, shaded groves.

We stripped out of our clothes and waded into the pleasantly cool water, tearing up handfuls of the grassy stuff as we went. We found a rocky ledge at the base of the short waterfall where we could kneel waist-high in the water, and there we scrubbed the dirt off each other. Then we moved out onto the grassy bank and stretched out, letting the sun warm and dry us.

The forest around us was alive with sounds—insects, birds, the chittering of small animals. We could hear the muttering of sha'um and, too distant to concern us, the grunting sounds of a boar-like creature Keeshah had warned us to avoid.

Tarani sighed. "I could wish to stay here, Rikardon," she said. "I did not believe such beauty could exist. Indomel, the Ra'ira, Kä—they seem so distant and unimportant here."

I felt the same way. I wanted to live here with Tarani, Keeshah, and Yayshah, to see the cubs born and grown, perhaps to bring up children and cubs together. No roguelords, no politics, no complex destiny to clutter up our lives.

I let the fantasy claim me for a few seconds, then the sound of nearby movement brought me sharply back to reality.

Keeshah? I asked. *Is that you behind us?*

I guard, he said.

"Where is Yayshah?" I asked Tarani.

"In the lair," she answered, after a moment. "She misses Keeshah." Tarani looked at me questioningly.

"He's protecting us," I said. "Tarani, we—I have interrupted an important natural cycle. As long as I'm in the Valley . . ."

I didn't have to finish the thought. "I merely dreamed of staying, my love," Tarani said. "We must go soon, and not only for the sake of the sha'um."

"The search for Ka will be more difficult without Lonna," I said, remembering the joyful moment when the white bird had come to Lingis with Tarani's letter.

Tarani reached across the distance between us and put her hand in mine. "I am glad to hear you speak of Ka," she said. "I had feared you would argue again for Rika as the needed symbol, especially since it is with us again."

"I . . . believe the other sword is what we need," I said.

Tarani stared at me as though she could hear what I hadn't said: *for your sakes, Tarani and Antonia*. I braced myself on my elbow and looked down at her.

"We have to go, but not right away," I said. "After what we've been through, we deserve a little peace, some time together."

I reached for her, and she came hungrily into my arms.

We touched and learned and loved, together but alone, a less wild but no less passionate joining. We slept, woke, accomplished the mundane chore of washing our clothes, bathed and laughed and made love. For the rest of that day we were free and natural creatures, with no thought but to exist and enjoy one another. When night came, we returned to the lair. The sha'um hunted in the early evening, but returned in the night. Tarani and I woke inside a cozy nest of fur, between the curled, sleeping bodies of Keeshah and Yayshah.

Keeshah and Yayshah walked with us into the western hills of the Valley, toward the Alkhum Pass. Other sha'um appeared along the way to make unfriendly comments, but no one stepped forward to challenge our escorts.

As we moved through the forest—taking a route which zigzagged through sunlight and shadow and avoided the worst patches of thorny briars—I felt the peace fading and the world closing in on me again. I was aware of being dressed for "civilization" with boots and weapons, a moneybelt and a waterpouch.

I felt a poignant regret at leaving the Valley, but no real hesitation. I had intruded on Keeshah's world; I appreciated his tolerance, but I knew I had to go back to my own. I tried desperately to prepare myself to leave him again. It wouldn't be as bad this time, with our link active and the knowledge—absolute sureness—that he would come to me as soon as he could leave his family. But I would miss him.

I held Tarani's hand and reached out to Keeshah's mind as we walked. I sensed restlessness and anxiety in the sha'um, and I attributed it to concern for our safety and anticipation of missing me. I could hardly offer the cat comfort which eluded me, so I merely tried to keep warm, caring thoughts at the forefront of my mind.

We reached a point which seemed to be a natural place to part, where the forest was giving way to patchy green hillside that rose sharply toward the Alkhum Pass. I turned to face Keeshah, to say goodbye . . . and reeled backward as if from a physical blow.

The sha'um released all his anxiety in a flood of garbled pleading, anger, and confusion.

*Stay.
*Others will kill.
*I guard.
*Female; cubs; need me.
*Can't guard and hunt too.
*I will come.
*Cubs; must stay in the Valley.
*Rikardon; desert; die alone.
*Female; soon too clumsy to hunt; die alone.
*Stay.
*Intrudes; female; cubs; important; right.
*No thinking here; lonely.
*No female outside; lonely.
*Female . . .
*Cubs . . .
*Rikardon . . .

Yayshah approached Keeshah and stretched out her head to lay her dark throat across his tawny shoulders. Keeshah pressed into her caress briefly, then sidestepped with a snarl and aimed a clawless swat at her nose.

The female sank instantly into a crouch, her ears flattening. She growled, and was answered with a roar. She lunged past Keeshah, took several long jumps up the hillside, then turned

159

and planted all four feet firmly. The fur behind her head lifted in a mane, and her lips trembled back from her teeth, exposing the wide, sharp tusks at either side of her mouth. A sound so low that I wasn't sure I heard it floated down the hillside to us.

Keeshah's mane lifted; his tail fluffed and whipped back and forth as he paced indecisively, keeping his eye on the female.

They don't need a mindlink to understand each other, I thought to myself.

Tarani whirled on me. "Keeshah can't leave the Valley!" she screamed, and started pounding on my chest with her fists.

I grabbed her shoulders. "Tarani!" I shouted. "Is that you or Yayshah talking?"

A look of understanding replaced the scowl on her face, and she brought one hand up to touch her forehead. "I—It's difficult to separate myself from her in this, Rikardon. It touches such a basic need—mate, family, all her survival instincts are involved.

"Is Keeshah truly thinking of coming with us? Leaving her?"

"He doesn't know what he wants," I said. "I think I really fouled up his life, forcing the link to become active again this early. He can't quite regain the 'animal' state he was in, but that same instinctive need to protect his family is still very strong. His loyalty to me, and his loyalty to her—he's caught between them."

I'm sorry, Keeshah, I said, but only to myself. *I didn't know I was going to precipitate an identity crisis. If there had been any other way to get out of the Well of Darkness alive, I would have taken it.*

"He loves you both," Tarani summarized it. "Oh, Keeshah, how hard this must be for you..."

She walked over to the pale-furred sha'um, who paused in surprise at her approach. She smoothed the fur along his wide jaw, then put her arms around his neck.

Keeshah twisted his head around and rubbed his ear against Tarani's shoulder. Then he pulled away and crouched down to the ground—in the mounting crouch.

I will come, he told me, the tone of his thought final.

I felt as confused as Keeshah had been. I was delighted (with, I admit, a touch of gloating) that Keeshah had chosen me above Yayshah. Tarani's gesture had been a reminder of

160

friendship—a relationship of choice, unavailable in the Valley, where circumstance and instinct ruled. Keeshah cared deeply for his mate, but the fact that his mate was Yayshah was a biological accident—it had simply happened that way. Keeshah's bonding to Markasset could be put into almost the same category—that it was mere accident that Keeshah had been the cub whom Markasset first met in the Valley.

But Keeshah had lost Markasset in the Kapiral Desert. He had consciously and rationally accepted me as his friend, and I had shared more of his life, his thoughts, his feelings, his being than Yayshah could match. His feelings for her stemmed from a limited, if powerful, aspect of his personality. Having experienced a larger dimension through Markasset and me, he could no longer content himself with anything less. For the second time, he chose me, and I was glad.

Yet I sensed his lingering concern for Yayshah. I knew little of the habits of wild sha'um, but in that brief, blurry onslaught of feelings from Keeshah, I had seen his image of her future. No other male would take his place. She would grow too large to hunt successfully. When the time came for her cubs to be born, she would be alone and feeble. I hated that picture almost as much as Keeshah did.

From the hillside came a long, high-pitched roar. Yayshah launched herself downward and came to a quivering halt, crouched and snarling, not three yards from where Tarani stood, tense and watchful, close to Keeshah.

"She knows Keeshah has decided to leave," Tarani said in a dazed, singsong voice. "She is frightened, and sad—Great Zanek, how much she cares for Keeshah. He is strong, and handsome, a fine hunter. Their cubs—there will be three—will have his high shoulders and great strength. The cubs—will they live if she cannot even hunt for herself?"

Tarani crossed the space to the female, her voice a moan of grief. She knelt beside Yayshah, who trembled at the girl's touch but still watched Keeshah with a wild expression.

I felt rooted to the ground, mesmerized by Tarani's recital of Yayshah's agony.

"She has always known that Keeshah is different—how proud she was when he chose her!—but until we came to the Valley, she didn't know what had caused the difference. She knows, now, that he has seen the world outside. She has looked into my mind and seen my memory of Keeshah, and is even more proud of him. She knows his difference has touched her, too.

"He must go among men again, and she cannot deny him because touching me has shown her what he would give up to stay with her. She is curious, afraid, needful. She wants Keeshah with her. She wants her lair—it took her a long time to get it just right. But more than anything, she wants Keeshah with her when the cubs come..."

The distant look faded from Tarani's eyes and she stared at me in amazement. "Rikardon, she is thinking of coming with us!"

I didn't question it.

Keeshah, I said quickly. *The female wants to come along.*

I felt relief from him, mixed with uncertainty. *True?* he asked. When I had confirmed it, he asked hesitantly: *All right?*

You're asking me for permission? I said. *Of course it's all right with me. The decision is up to you and Yayshah.*

Keeshah stood up and moved slowly toward Yayshah. Tarani stepped out of the way as the female rose to meet him. The sha'um touched noses, then Keeshah rubbed his mate, starting cheek to cheek and moving past her, leaning against her, until only their tail tips were touching.

I joined Tarani and put my arm around her waist. "Will Yaysha come with us?" I whispered.

"I do not know," Tarani whispered back. "It is a more difficult decision for her. No female has ever left the Valley, cubs have never been born or nurtured anywhere else. To leave now goes against all her instincts."

"Yet she wants to," I said.

"Yes, for Keeshah and for me." Her voice revealed an awe that was totally familiar to me. The friendship of a sha'um is a humbling experience. "I never considered it, Rikardon, and I would not have asked it of her. But I do want her with me." Her eyes lit up. "It is a petty thought, I know—but I... it would please me to be the first woman to bring a female sha'um from the Valley."

I turned her to face me.

"Another symbol of your 'right to rule' in Eddarta?" I asked.

"Perhaps," she said. "But not one which would replace the second sword.

162

"Perhaps it is only that I wish to be what Vasklar named me, an agent of change." Her mood lightened suddenly. "And perhaps I only wish to see Thymas's face, if I should have occasion to ride a female sha'um into Thagorn."

I smiled at the image. Thymas, young as he was, was a dyed-in-the-wool traditionalist. It would be easier for his father, the Lieutenant of the Sharith, to accept a woman Rider than it would be for Thymas—even if, or possibly *especially* if that Rider were Tarani.

"If she comes with us, we'll see Thagorn again soon," I said. "There are sha'um there, and free-running vlek for game. It's the most natural place I can think of, outside the Valley, for her cubs to be born."

"*If* she comes with us," Tarani said. "She still has not decided—and I do not think she will decide until forced to."

Keeshah seemed to have the same thing in mind. He touched his nose once more to Yayshah's, then came to crouch down in front of us.

Go, he said. *Now.*

That last was said impatiently, and Keeshah had my sympathy. The suspense was about to kill me, too.

Will the female come with us? I asked him as I mounted. I would never again take for granted—if, indeed, I ever had done so—the security and pleasure of Keeshah's muscular back beneath me.

She must choose, he said. *I go.*

Tarani stepped close to mount behind me. Yayshah made an odd sound, shook her head vigorously twice, then ran over to stretch her neck across my back to touch Tarani's chest with her muzzle.

"She *will* come with us," Tarani said, in an emotion-choked voice. "She wants me to—to ride her. Oh, Rikardon, is it safe? For the cubs, I mean? For her to carry my weight?"

"I'd say she's the best judge of that," I said, and ducked as Tarani scrambled over Keeshah's back in her eagerness to get to Yayshah.

Tarani stroked the dark fur between Yayshah's wide-set eyes, and I discovered for the first time that there was more difference between Keeshah and his mate than size and coloring. The female was proportionally narrower across her shoulders, and her muzzle was pointed more sharply. And the curve of her belly was rounder.

Noticeably rounder.

With hands and words and mind, Tarani guided Yayshah into a version of the mounting crouch—she didn't want her weight to pressure the unborn cubs—and mounted carefully. Yayshah stood up, balancing Tarani's weight awkwardly, and paced around a bit, getting the feel of carrying a rider.

She's going to come with us, Keeshah, I said happily.

Desert? he questioned worriedly.

No, I promise you we'll wait until the cubs are born to go into the desert.

Good, he said, and surged to his feet. *Go now. Home?*

He meant Raithskar, and the stone house in Thanasset's back yard, where Keeshah had spent most of his life.

Not yet, I said. *We'll go to Thagorn first.*

As we headed south, Tarani asked: "Where are we going? The Alkhum Pass is west of us, is it not?"

"I told you how hard a crossing it is," I said. "I wouldn't ask a pregnant lady to go through that. We'll visit Thagorn, instead."

"What about Worfit? Could he not be waiting for us at the edge of the Valley?"

"He might," I admitted, thinking about Worfit for the first time in what seemed ages. "But those men with him were none too eager to tackle one sha'um—I don't think he'll get much support for a plan to attack *two* sha'um, do you?"

We rode on in silence for a while, moving slowly so that Yayshah could become accustomed to Tarani.

Woman knows female? Keeshah asked me.

Yes, Tarani talks to Yayshah the way I talk to you, I agreed.

Why?

I sighed.

I don't really know, Keeshah. I think it has something to do with you and me being together, and with Yayshah being your mate and Tarani mine.

Woman have cubs?

I laughed, and Tarani jumped at the sudden sound.

"Keeshah just asked me if you were pregnant," I said, then stopped short. "Uh—you're not, are you?"

She stared at Yayshah's left ear. "I would not have allowed...I was not fertile," she finished awkwardly. "This is not the time to think of such things, Rikardon. There is too much to be done. The sword. Eddarta. The safety of the Ra'ira." She held out her hand, and I took it. Riding this slowly, we assumed a position close to a normal sitting position. "You knew, long ago, that it was for you to safeguard the Ra'ira. I share that need, that duty, and I will not be free until it is done."

You will not be free, I countered to myself, *until you hold a steel sword in your hands and reconcile Antonia with Tarani.*

"Afterward..." She let the word hang in the air.

"Afterward, we'll find a place like this," I said, waving to indicate the tall trees and dappled, leaf-covered ground, "and let our children get to know our cubs." I squeezed her hand. "Ready to try a run?"

Her face lit up.

We lay forward on the sha'um, gripping their shoulders for security. Keeshah had been waiting for the chance. He sprang forward and stretched out, and trees seemed to fly by us. I watched Tarani and Yayshah long enough to tell that they were getting the hang of it, then I closed my eyes, pressed my face into Keeshah's fur, and let myself join him in the pleasure of the run.

I missed you, Keeshah, I told him, knowing that he could hear more emotion than the words could convey.

Female slow, he said, and it was more a boast than a complaint—and it wasn't, as far as I could see from Tarani riding, eyes closed, shoulder to shoulder with me, very true.

Yayshah's keeping up with us, I said, puzzled.

I felt a wash of good feeling from him, the basic physical joy of the run mingling with contentment. For a moment, I studied his pace, the way his body moved beneath me.

Keeshah, you're matching her, aren't you, so she won't fall behind?

Belong together, he said.

Yes we do, I thought. *All of us.*

END PROCEEDINGS:
INPUT SESSION FOUR

　　—I withdraw our minds from the All-Mind, and now yours
is free of mine . . .

　　—Are you well? You tremble.

　　—Yes, Recorder. I tremble. Obilin's death, the satisfaction
of it . . .

　　—If I may speak as a person, and not as a Recorder?

　　—Of course.

　　—Were I to have held the knife at that moment, the result
would have been the same. Obilin was truly an evil man.

　　—Thank you for saying that, Recorder. Now I must go . . .

　　—Yes, the Record is a user of time. When you are ready
again, call upon me.

ABOUT THE AUTHORS

RANDALL GARRETT, a veteran science fiction and fantasy writer, and VICKI ANN HEYDRON, a newcomer to the field, met in 1975 in the California home of their mutual agent, Tracy E. Blackstone. Within a year, they had decided to begin working together and, in December 1978, they were married.

Currently, they are living in Austin, Texas, where they are working on the Gandalara novels, of which *The Steel of Raithskar* is the first, *The Glass of Dyskornis* second, *The Bronze of Eddarta* third, and *The Well of Darkness* fourth.

Coming in May, 1984 . . .
The thrilling fifth volume in the *Gandalara Cycle*

THE SEARCH
FOR KA

by Randall Garrett and Vicki Ann Heydron

Rikardon and Tarani, along with Keeshah and Yayshah, set off on their quest for Ka. There, they must seek out the second steel sword and return it to Eddarta where Tarani can lay claim to the leadership of the Lords and the awesome powers of the Ra'ira. Along the way, they will face the gravest dangers and Tarani will meet a destiny she never dreamed of.

Read THE SEARCH FOR KA, on sale May 15, 1984. Buy any of the earlier books in the *Gandalara Cycle* you might have missed wherever Bantam paperbacks are sold or by using the handy coupon below:

"Unput-downable! A rollicking good read."
—Anne McCaffrey

BRONWYN'S BANE

by Elizabeth Scarborough

Bronwyn, Crown Princess of Argonia, was born under an unlucky star. Not only was she a strapping, awkward, hot-tempered girl ill-suited to palace life, but she'd been cursed at birth with a spell that made her tell nothing but lies. When war breaks out, Bronwyn is sent to the home of her cousin Carole, who'd inherited the gift of musical magic from her hearthwitch mother and minstrel father. But where Bronwyn went, trouble followed, and soon she and Carole were hip-deep in sorcerers, sirens, sea serpents, mercenary mages, and malevolent monsters. Joined by a princess-turned-swan and a less-than-fearless Gypsy lad, the pair set off on an adventure-filled quest to end the war, heal a blighted land, and lift Bronwyn's bane once and for all.

Read BRONWYN'S BANE and Elizabeth Scarborough's other novels, on sale wherever Bantam paperbacks are sold, or use the handy coupon below for ordering: